TWO SPINSTERS AND A SWINDLER

TWO SPINSTERS AND A MURDER MYSTERY

EVE TARRINGTON

Copyright © 2024 by Eve Tarrington

All rights reserved.

No part of this book may be reproduced in any form or by any electronic or mechanical means, including information storage and retrieval systems, without written permission from the author, except for the use of brief quotations in a book review.

For my youngest family members. Welcome to the world!

ALSO BY EVE TARRINGTON

Two Spinsters and a Corpse

Two Spinsters and a Duel

Two Spinsters and a Madman

Two Spinsters Books 1-3 Box Set

Two Spinsters and a Thief

Two Spinsters and an Assassin

Two Spinsters and a Villain

1

When Judith saw her fiancé standing at the end of the street, she prayed that he was not an apparition. It helped that Judith had just emerged from a wedding, so most of the crowd was focused on the wedding party, not the man standing some distance away. In fact, the activity of the happy newlyweds behind them engaged the full attention of everyone except for Judith and her friend Louisa-Margaretta.

The latter, understanding the nature of the moment, squeezed Judith's hand before walking away.

Though she was in company on the church steps, Judith felt quite alone as Morgan approached her. He began to run as he drew near, and by the time he spoke, he was quite out of breath.

"Judith." He took her gloved hand in his. "Oh, Judith."

She could not take her eyes from his face. He looked concerned, but he was there before her, just as he had been in all of her dreams.

"Everyone thought you had died," she managed,

squeezing his hand through her glove, wishing she could feel his skin and be absolutely sure he was real.

His brow wrinkled as if he were confused. "Did you believe me dead?"

"No," she whispered. "I knew that you had not died. I could feel it. And if none of the fine lords were willing to send a delegation, I was on the point of going to France myself."

"Dear Judith," said Morgan, and something like a sob escaped his lips. He clutched her hand tighter.

Judith had never wished more earnestly for an embrace, but even in her very great joy, she was cognizant of the London street on which she found herself and of the presence of friends and family members quite near her.

So she and Morgan simply stood before each other, the irrepressible smiles on their faces mingling with tears. He wore a set of clothes she had never seen on him before, and she could tell that his hands were leathery and worn.

He took out a handkerchief she did not recognize, passed it over to her without a word, and after touching her eyes furtively, she handed it back to him.

"What happened?" she asked.

He did not let go of her hand as he told her the story of all that had befallen him, and when he had finished, Judith's only thought was that they should have married long before that ordeal had started.

She was half tempted to go back into the church and tell the vicar who had performed the previous ceremony to do another one, for she never intended to be parted from Morgan ever again.

"Oh, my love," Judith said when he had finished. "I do understand. But let us never again undertake such travels separately."

He managed a half smile. "Of course! You have still told me nothing of your time in Russia."

Judith sighed. "That is quite a story in itself, though I daresay not quite as terrifying as what happened to you."

Morgan shook his head. "What happened to me is in the past. Though it was a trial, I am not ashamed of it and now have only to treasure the blessings of the future."

"Of course," she breathed, and for a moment, neither spoke. They were still unable to embrace, and their surroundings bore little resemblance to Wycliff Castle's secluded orchards and grounds, the site of their former courtship.

"You were very brave," Judith said. "And now, thanks be to God, it is over."

2

Judith's family was not nearly as understanding when she told them of Morgan's troubles.

Her aunt Leah, sitting with a straight back by the fire, was the first to voice doubt. "So, he claims that he and his party were robbed and that one of those gentlemen killed a robber?"

"It was an accident," Judith hastened to explain. "The man was only defending himself, truly. But he hit the highwayman's head most violently, and the man fell. The other men scattered."

"Then they should have just ridden on," Miriam said decidedly. "They probably could have made it all the way back to England."

Miriam was embroidering a handkerchief, keeping it near a candle so she could see her intricate work. She had always made a habit of neglecting her workbasket, but perhaps the time she had spent as the eldest child present with the family had changed her. Though Judith was vexed with Miriam for doubting Morgan's word, she was secretly pleased to see the small, even stitches her sister was making.

"If I were set upon by highwaymen, I should not leave!" said Aaron, running in. "I should stay and fight!"

At ten years old, Aaron was definitely too young for such an account, and Judith had gone to some trouble to ensure that none of her brothers heard anything about her fiancé's troubles.

"Off to bed," said Aunt Leah, shepherding Aaron out of the room.

"But Moses has stolen my nightcap!"

"Then you'd best take it back from him, hadn't you?" said Aunt Leah.

"Does Mr Ramsbury understand how you worried for him, dear?" asked Mr St Clair as they waited for Aunt Leah to return.

Judith's father was thin, but Judith was pleased to see that he appeared to be in very good health. After she had left the country nearly a year ago, she had tried to ascertain his well-being from letters, which was rather difficult. But she could see for herself that he was quite healthy, and he appeared to be happy to have his family gathered about him. Aunt Leah, his sister, often came for long visits, and since Judith was home, she knew that her father would feel relieved from the burden of worrying about her.

"He knew quite well that everyone would be concerned," said Judith. "But he and his companion could not very well reveal their identities. They were afraid they would be killed themselves."

Aunt Leah came back in, sweeping her long skirts out of the way as she took her seat by the fire again.

Judith, who had been pretending to work at some embroidery, put it down in her lap.

"Truly," she said, "Mr Ramsbury and his friend had no choice. It was very fortunate for them that a farmer took pity on them both and ended up helping them hide with his cousin some ten miles away."

Only Mr St Clair nodded. "Of course, my dear. And now, what does he propose to do?"

Judith blinked. "I'm sorry, Papa?"

"Well, I believe he will abandon his diplomatic pursuits," said Mr St Clair. "And I do not blame the boy, to be sure. Now that Napoleon Bonaparte has been defeated, the need for diplomats is not nearly so great."

Judith bristled at hearing her beloved referred to as a "boy," but she kept her countenance serene. "I believe the same, Papa."

"Well, then? What is it to be?"

"If he wishes to be a curate, there will be a post open here soon," said Aunt Leah, a broad smile on her face.

"Mr Barnwell is leaving?" asked Judith, genuinely shocked. She could not keep her disappointment from showing. Her father's health had been troubled before the arrival of Mr Barnwell, but after the young curate took on some of his duties, there had been a marked improvement. Without any assistance, Judith's father would have to take on all of the onerous work of a busy rector once again, and he might find it very taxing. Though, of course, he would never complain. That was always the trouble.

Mr St Clair smiled, and in his joy, he looked rather like his sister. Though Leah St Clair had the same piercing blue eyes as her brother, the resemblance was not very marked. Where she was tall and strong, he was given to intellectual pursuits and meek by nature. He was a fast walker but growing a bit stooped with age, and he was exceedingly peaceful by nature.

"Well," he said. "Miriam, my dear, would you like to tell Judith your news?"

"Mr Barnwell and I are engaged," Miriam said, her tone clipped. "He is to start a new position in the new year."

Mr St Clair smiled. "An old friend of mine is leaving a living vacant," he said. "Judith, you remember Mr Fitzroy? As you know, he is not far from us at all. He thought his flock would take to a young man a bit better if they made the change just at the beginning of the new year. So the living will be Mr Barnwell's as of Christmas Day, but he and his bride will not leave Derbyshire until January."

Judith found herself deeply surprised, but she knew the proper thing to say. "I wish you much joy, Miriam."

"Thank you," said Miriam, but Judith thought her sister did not look at all pleased. Miriam had set her work down in her lap and was glaring out the window, unwilling to even look at Judith.

"Well," said their father, "we all ought to get to bed. There is plenty of work to be done tomorrow."

"Yes," said Judith faintly, though she did not quite know what her work should be.

And her fiancé, it would appear, had the very same problem. He had returned to England but had not yet determined how he was to spend his days.

And unless Judith was much mistaken, her father did not approve.

3

Louisa-Margaretta Haddington could not bear to wait for the Christmas guests. She had no wish to see any of them, so she stayed in the music room and played on the pianoforte.

The aria that came to her was one that Ivo Solier had written. When she was far from his presence, Louisa-Margaretta was able to think on him more fondly than she ever had in Russia or London.

He was an impressive figure, though he had the French curse of snobbery, and his looks were not at all bad. Louisa-Margaretta's only trouble was that she did not love him. Had she listened to her mother rather than following her own heart, she would almost certainly be married to that gentleman.

And that would mean she would be spending Christmas in London or perhaps even Paris, with people at the center of the operatic world. They would all be learned, clever, but Louisa-Margaretta's wealth and beauty would mean that she could hold her own in such a crowd.

Instead, she was in a drafty Derbyshire castle, trying to

avoid her mother's second cousin and that woman's family. Louisa-Margaretta had been the only Haddington child to live at home for nearly a decade, and she envied her elder brothers their homes and freedom. For them, marriage was not required for an escape.

Louisa-Margaretta stopped playing, put her head down on the piano, and moaned.

"Louisa-Margaretta? Are you unwell?"

Judith came striding into the room and took a seat next to her friend.

"I am quite well," said Louisa-Margaretta, "but I dread this holiday. It is nothing more than an excuse for my mother to bore us to tears with guests and prayer."

"It will be a very happy Christmas," said Judith, though her frown betrayed her doubts.

"Well, at least we may hope that nobody will be poisoned or shoved into a canal," said Louisa-Margaretta. "If we all escape with our lives, I suppose we can consider it an improvement on previous years."

Judith wore a pale-green gown. Instead of commenting on Louisa-Margaretta's remarks, she looked nervously at her well-mended gloves. "Do I look silly? I shall feel very shabby next to your guests, I am sure."

Louisa-Margaretta shook her head. It was very unlike Judith to complain about what she was wearing, but then, the holiday was to be a rather important one for her.

"I always think such pale colors do not look well on a lady with brown eyes," said Judith. "This gown suited Miriam much better."

Louisa-Margaretta gave a wicked grin. "Do I think that dear Cousin Morgan will like it, do you mean? Judith, you know quite well that he liked you in your poorest rags. Quakers like my cousin are hopelessly attached to that odd 'plain dress' custom. If he could tolerate the sort of horrid dresses we had to wear when we were working in Essex, he will be extremely impressed with your gown."

"I hope everyone there is doing well," said Judith. "I suppose it does not surprise you that I miss having an occupation."

Louisa-Margaretta considered that. "There were benefits, I suppose," she said, remembering how interesting her days had been. "Though I prefer not having to chase madmen through the woods. Imagine how difficult that would be here in Derbyshire!"

Judith looked down. "You don't suppose they are in need of anyone, do you?" she asked, referring to the asylum in Essex. "I was thinking of inquiring, but usually, they allow married couples to live together only if they are the superintendents of the entire place."

Louisa-Margaretta raised her eyebrows. "Yes, and that did not seem a very pleasant role. Judith, don't even think of returning! Does not my cousin have some alternative in mind?"

Judith smiled, but she did not laugh. "He says nothing of a profession," she fretted. "Do you think your father could be convinced to hire him?"

Louisa-Margaretta shook her head, playing a series of rather pleasing chords with her left hand while fixing her hair with her right. She had asked Harriet to help her make it stylish, but the weight of it simply felt burdensome. "Cousin Morgan has no head for business at all. Papa would only laugh at me. Besides, does he not have a fortune of his own?"

Judith frowned. "He gave a great deal of it away. Which I support, of course. The Quakers have certainly been in need of his generosity."

Louisa-Margaretta scoffed. "That is a problem I would only ever expect you and Cousin Morgan to have, dear Judith. Becoming paupers for your own good hearts! Well, never fear. Between what he has left and what he can earn, I am sure you will manage."

"Without a profession, he can earn little," said Judith. "We have very great need of my dowry, in fact, but if he is not working, I am afraid my father will not give his consent."

Louisa-Margaretta raised her eyebrows. "What is your fortune to be, then, Judith? Do give me the exact amount."

The young woman in the pale-green gown blushed. She began tidying the sheets of parchment that Louisa-Margaretta had piled on top of the pianoforte.

"It is not a fortune, only some money he hoped to settle on me," she said. "It amounts to five thousand pounds."

Louisa-Margaretta shrieked. "Five thousand pounds, Judith! Lord, your family must live on nothing. How could he have managed to save half so much?"

Judith fingered the material of her gown, swallowing. "To own the truth, I have no idea," she said quietly. "I am not sure if it is even right for me to take the money."

Louisa-Margaretta shrugged. "Would that I had your fortitude, Judith. If I had a fiancé whom I loved, along with a rather healthy sum of money, I would marry in a shot."

Judith's face fell. "Oh, Louisa-Margaretta. I am quite sure that—"

"I will find someone suitable? I highly doubt that," said Louisa-Margaretta archly. "With two broken engagements behind me, and at the age of eight and twenty? No, my dear."

There was noise outside the window. It was unmistakable—the guests were arriving.

"Perhaps..." said Judith.

"Perhaps there will be someone suitable in this party? I highly doubt it," said Louisa-Margaretta. "Though, knowing my mother, it is very possible that there is someone in the bunch whom she wishes me to marry."

With that unhappy thought in her head, Louisa-Margaretta rose to her feet and went to greet the guests.

4

When Judith and Louisa-Margaretta met the party, Judith realised that there was nobody among them whom her friend could marry. But she found herself rather relieved. Perhaps without a suitor, Louisa-Margaretta would be pleasanter to the guests. She always had a tendency to spend a bit too much time with the handsome gentlemen, neglecting those whom she considered unsightly or boring.

Judith, by contrast, was able to be pleasant without a great effort. As the daughter of the rector, she was ever conscious of her position. And since she had become officially engaged to a relative of Mrs Haddington, she also had the shame of being considered an interloper. She was quite eager to make it clear that she remained humble and unaffected, though her fortunes had certainly changed.

"Did you have a pleasant journey?" she asked the newcomers after trying her utmost to make out all their names, but nobody appeared to have heard her. As near as Judith could tell, the guests consisted of a young couple, the Blackmores, along with Mrs Blackmore's parents and sister.

Their surname was Guppy. Young Mr Blackmore's sister had joined the party for the holiday, as had Mrs Crampton, a friend of the family.

"I'm going to go lie down," said Mrs Nancy Blackmore, one of the younger guests, without acknowledging that Judith had spoken. She was in a certain condition, though it seemed absurd to Judith to speak in such euphemisms when Mrs Blackmore's belly was so large that the young woman's "condition" could not have possibly been mistaken for anything other than pregnancy. "That last carriage ride nearly did me in."

The young wife got no support from Mr Reuben Blackmore, her husband, who only sighed. Mrs Blackmore's mother, Mrs Guppy, seemed more concerned about her youngest daughter. She hardly reacted when the elder one said she was heading to her room to rest.

"We all ought to eat soon," she said. "Dear Jessie never eats enough."

The young woman she was speaking of scowled, and Judith suppressed a smile. Jessie Guppy, while thin, did not look as if she were starving.

Mrs Crampton, the elderly friend of the Guppy family who had accompanied them, touched Mrs Guppy's arm. "Your Jessie will be fine, but you must eat something yourself, Mrs Blackmore. You've had almost nothing all day."

Mrs Blackmore sniffed. "I do feel rather faint. But we ought to wait until all the parties have arrived, then we shall dine together."

Mr Guppy gave a jovial smile. "Derbyshire is rather far, what? All of this traveling has nearly done us in."

"I hope you will find that your journey is well worth it," said Mrs Haddington in soothing tones.

Miss Rose Blackmore, sister of the scowling Mr Reuben

Blackmore, gave a broad smile. "Oh, this beautiful place is the talk of London. I am sure all our friends are quite jealous!"

"Always a good enough reason to come here," sniffed Louisa-Margaretta. "Making one's friends jealous, though if they were to experience an actual Derbyshire winter, they would not be nearly so keen."

Miss Blackmore, rather than taking offense, simply laughed. "Oh, how charming! Well, I do feel that many in London do not have the proper spirit for fighting through a winter like this one. But we shall simply have to make very good use of our cloaks."

Judith tried to think of a clever response, as Miss Blackmore seemed the sort of young lady whose conversation consisted of trading witty remarks, but she was spared by the next arrival.

Mr Morgan Ramsbury, Judith's fiancé, had shared one of the Haddingtons' coaches with a Mr Pembroke Lush. The two had traveled together from Manchester, with the Haddingtons sending the coach for them so they would not have to travel post. Though reliable, traveling post was a slow and cold way of making the journey, and around Christmas, it could feel akin to torture.

Judith hardly knew how to look when Morgan kissed her hand, a proper greeting for a visiting acquaintance. Their engagement was not a secret, of course, but she knew that Mrs Haddington disapproved.

Though Judith tried to speak with him as the party was welcomed into Wycliff Castle, Mrs Haddington shepherded him toward his room with the rest of the guests. Once everyone came down, it was already time to eat. Judith felt many flutterings of agony when she could neither be seated near her love at table nor find a moment to speak with him.

Louisa-Margaretta was also quiet, Miss Guppy rarely spoke, and Mr Haddington was his usual silent self. Mrs Blackmore had taken to her bed, Mrs Guppy was feeling unwell, and Mrs Crampton seemed to speak only in murmurs. That did not make for a very merry party.

When someone asked whether any of them had heard of Mostiania, Judith was relieved.

"I have not heard of it," she said, feeling a bit ashamed. Geography had always been one of her strengths, and after providing Miriam and all her brothers with so much instruction, she was surprised there was any place that was unknown to her, no matter how remote. "But I would love to hear more about it. Please, do tell me."

5

Mr Lush was more than happy to hold court at the dinner table, going on about his favourite subject. He was well traveled, and while he had a few stories of his time in Paris and Rome, the land that had captured his heart was plainly very different.

"Mostiania," he said. "It is at once the most beautiful country I have visited and by far the richest."

Louisa-Margaretta smirked. She was tempted to make a joke that she was also beautiful and rich, though she thought that sad little Jessy Guppy would not laugh, and she certainly could not say such a thing in front of the elderly Mrs Crampton.

"Do you go every year, then?" asked Papa, peering at Mr Lush with his dark eyes. He seldom contributed much to the conversation, but Louisa-Margaretta knew that he could not resist taking interest in a business proposition. "Seems rather expensive."

Mr Lush was only too happy to describe his journey. "Oh, it is! Over a month to get there and almost two to get back. And that is just for the journey to Buenos Aires. After that, one must get another boat. It is quite an ordeal."

Mr Haddington raised his eyebrows. "It would be easier to choose somewhere closer. Even getting to Manchester is inconvenient at times."

Louisa-Margaretta suppressed a laugh. Only her father would say something like that and remain unashamed. As if one could compare taking a carriage into Manchester with traveling to a far distant land by boat!

Mr Lush shook his head. "My dear sir, of course not! For Mositania is as yet pure, untamed, a wild land eminently suited for the right sort of cultivation."

Why is it that gentlemen always speak of these lands as if they are ladies? thought Louisa-Margaretta. *Rather vapid ladies, at that.*

"What do you intend to cultivate there, sir?" asked Mama.

Mr Lush's smile, which had been respectful when he was speaking to the man of the house, instantly became softer and rather condescending.

"Well, the plans are complex, madam," he said. "Gold will be a primary focus, but it is also excellent land for farming and tobacco. That will help support the mining operation."

"I'm always trying to get my son to learn more about farming," said Mr Guppy. "But I expect he's more interested in the gold! I can hardly blame him."

Mr Lush smiled. "Of course, of course. After having seen the riches of South America, I cannot blame anyone with an interest in extracting them. That has become my primary aim."

There were so many oddities in Mr Lush's speech. Louisa-Margaretta was quite sure that, like most travelers, he was leaving out many of the discomforts he had experienced. He said nothing of biting insects, for example, and she was sure that the "savage native inhabitants" could not be half so gentle as he claimed.

"It sounds rather dull to me," she said. "Tell me, did you visit any of the neighbouring territories on your last visit? Was anyone at war?"

Mr Guppy gave a snort. "That's all that ladies admire these days, war. I suppose you wish we had not vanquished Napoleon Bonaparte, Miss Haddington? I confess, I prefer to sleep each night knowing his henchmen are not coming to our shores, but perhaps that is my own peculiarity."

Louisa-Margaretta's smile was broad. "I only wondered what Mostiania's neighbours were like," she said brightly. "After all, we are so very near France yet not like it in any way."

"Have you been to France?" asked Mr Blackmore.

Louisa-Margaretta scowled. "No." She had been to Russia, but her parents were still upset that she had gone at all. She knew better than to mention her year there in company. Mr Blackmore's remark reminded her, most cruelly, of the operatic life she had given up in Paris. Perhaps living with Mr Solier as his wife would have been a trial, but she was fond of the Duke of Ormonde, and she knew that he had gone to the continent with one of his companions. They might even then be waltzing through a French ballroom, not listening to some bore go on about his business prospects.

Mr Lush gave her his smile, sweet as treacle. "There is no cause, surely. You ladies ought to stay in England. After all, someone must tend to the hearth while the men are away! And though beautiful Mostiania is as lovely a land as I have ever seen, the journey is not suitable for a lady."

"I can assure you—" said Louisa-Margaretta, ready to risk her parents' approbation and describe the cramped sea voyage to and from St Petersburg. But Mama got there before her.

"My daughter is of an unusually adventurous disposition," Mrs Haddington said swiftly. "Indeed, she loves hunting. That is one reason we have seen fit to organise a hunt while everyone is here, if the weather suits! Perhaps we could make those plans now."

The rest of the dinner passed largely without incident, though Louisa-Margaretta scowled during a great deal of it. It did not escape her that Mr Lush spoke most with her father, then Mr Guppy and Mr Blackmore, and following that, with Cousin Morgan. It was by virtue of their material wealth, then, that he valued them. But he was either very stubborn or very stupid, because he did not think to approach Louisa-Margaretta or her mother, apparently believing them to have no influence at all over the respected Mr Haddington and his business interests.

By the time the dinner ended and the ladies and gentlemen separated, Louisa-Margaretta was thankful to be rid of him.

6

After dinner, Judith was with the ladies. Though typically she would have been happy, perhaps even relieved to be spared Mr Lush's loud boasts about his travels, that evening, she longed for Morgan's company. For months, they had written to each other, and for years, they had been on the edge of marriage! It was maddening.

Not for the first time, Judith wished she were the sort of young woman who might just rush off and marry in Scotland without her family's blessing. Were that the case, she would never have rejected Morgan's suit years ago, and they might well be married with a child or two.

And nothing to live on, she reminded herself. They required either an impressive profession for the husband or the dowry of the wife. Without either, there was no way forward for them.

"This is a welcome change from the London gatherings," said Miss Blackmore, taking a seat beside Judith and smiling animatedly. "At some of those parties, I scarcely got to speak to any of the other ladies! Too much noise and too many people."

"I am sure it was exciting," said Judith, and her companion nodded sagely.

"It was, rather," said Miss Blackmore, her beautiful dimples showing again as she grinned. "But the longer one remains unmarried, the worse it gets!"

"Indeed," said Judith, her stomach lurching as she thought about her feeble attempts to win her father's blessing for her marriage. "There is such a great deal of pressure on young ladies to marry and to marry well!"

Miss Blackmore only laughed. "Well, my mama was never as concerned about such things. Dear Reuben is happy enough to feed me, and even in these late months, Nancy has not yet grown to hate my company. No, I speak of the proposals!"

Judith blinked. "The proposals?"

"Oh yes," said Miss Blackmore. "All of the gentlemen who wished to marry me! And after the most slender of acquaintances too."

Judith looked about. She was not quite sure what the other ladies would think of Miss Blackmore's story. Mrs Haddington, Mrs Guppy, and Mrs Crampton were in one corner, speaking in gentle tones. Young Mrs Blackmore still kept to her room. Louisa-Margaretta was sitting at the piano with Miss Guppy, who glared in Judith's direction.

Judith gave Louisa-Margaretta and Miss Guppy a weak smile. The latter, she imagined, was probably just at an age where everything about family gatherings was vexing. And it was certainly not an easy journey, traveling for many days with her parents and the vivacious Miss Blackmore.

"The trouble with proposals," said Miss Blackmore,

seemingly pleased that Judith was hesitating to respond, "is that one simply can't go anywhere after one."

"I'm sorry," said Judith. "You mean one can't leave the house?"

Miss Blackmore's laugh was quite as pretty as the notes that Louisa-Margaretta was plucking out on the piano, and for the first time, Judith saw how easily a gentleman might lose his head over such a spirited and becoming young lady. It was no great wonder that Miss Blackmore had received multiple proposals.

"No, Miss St Clair," she said. "I may call you Judith, may I not?"

"Of course," said Judith, feeling that it was the only appropriate response.

"Dear Judith," said Miss Blackmore, "it has happened ever so many times! After a very brief acquaintance, a gentleman asks if I might wish to marry him."

"And?" said Judith.

Miss Blackmore shook her head. "I shall marry eventually, I suppose, but it will have to be the right sort of gentleman," she said mysteriously. "So in these cases, naturally, I said no."

"Naturally," said Judith, wondering if Miss Blackmore's speech was as unexamined as it seemed. Surely the young woman's education had not been so sorely neglected as to leave her in the belief that the topic was a good one for a new acquaintance?

"And after such a rejection, dear Judith, one simply cannot go on! No carriage rides, no small conversations, certainly no dancing. It is best for one to act as if one is not at all acquainted with the gentleman in question. And given the composition of Almack's, this can be quite a trial! For if one has to spurn at least one gentleman in each group of friends, well, very soon, it is difficult to speak with anyone at all."

Judith blinked. "Yes, I'm sure that is true."

"If only they were not so concerned about being honourable," mused Miss Blackmore. "Then again, if a gentleman knows he has overstepped, I suppose he really ought to make an offer of marriage. Otherwise, he shall be accused of giving one ideas about marriage without any intention behind them."

Judith nodded, not quite knowing how to answer.

"At any rate," said Miss Blackmore, "this gathering seems to have very few eligible bachelors, so I hope there will be less of that sort of thing. Mr Guppy and my brother have spent quite a bit of time with Mr Lush, and he does not seem at all interested in ladies. At least not in English ladies, at any rate! Perhaps he prefers the ladies in that country of his."

Judith felt ashamed that she could not quite remember the name of the territory. She, who had always prided herself on geography! "Mostiania?"

"Mositantia, I believe," said Miss Blackmore with perfect confidence, though Judith knew that was not quite correct. "At least, I am sure I have heard Mr Lush call it Mositantia, and I suppose he ought to know. Oh, speak of the devil!"

She waved as the gentlemen came through then turned back to Judith.

"How very rude of me," she said. "I have told you all about myself yet given you not a moment to speak. It is one of my grandest flaws, I am afraid! Do you have an admirer, Judith?"

Judith had never been a very skilled liar. Her eyes went straight to Morgan, who was approaching them.

Miss Blackmore grinned. "Say no more, you sly thing. So

this is the gentleman, eh? And I can tell he feels for you just as you feel for him."

When Judith could make no reply, Miss Blackmore nudged her away. "Of course you wish to speak with him! I shall go to the pianoforte straightaway and leave the two of you."

With an exaggerated wink, she sauntered over to the instrument, leaving Judith with a tiny smile as an exhausted Morgan sank down on the chair nearest hers.

"Miss Blackmore works quickly," he observed. "Still, I am sure that all of the Blackmore and Guppy visitors would have learned of our engagement soon enough."

Judith's smile disappeared, and Morgan leaned forward.

"You do not feel ashamed, surely," he said.

She shook her head. "No, only troubled. Miriam is to be married, apparently without any objections from Papa or Aunt Leah, and we have waited years! I cannot understand why my father will not yield."

Morgan did not look surprised. "He still insists that I find work before marrying you," he said, and Judith nodded.

"He will not hear of anything else," she said. "He is adamant about it, which is most unlike Papa."

Morgan sighed. "I cannot say that I blame him. I only wish my inquiries had been more satisfactory."

Judith's heart sank. "Nothing?"

Morgan pursed his lips. "Well, nothing yet, Judith. There are still a few possibilities. But until I have a very firm offer of employment, I will have nothing to share with your family."

"Perhaps we should have married in London," said Judith bitterly. "In coming back to Derbyshire, I have only allowed my father to create more obstacles."

Morgan sighed, and Judith wondered if he would touch

on the subject that had been troubling them both. For a moment, she thought he would get up and wander over to the corner where Miss Blackstone was amusing the younger ladies by pounding out a mazurka.

To his credit, he stayed. "Your dowry is the trouble," he said flatly. "I should never have been quite so foolish with my inheritance, and I also never imagined your father would be able to give so much."

"Yes," said Judith. "But if he will not give his consent, and there is no work to be had, then there is nothing for it. In many ways, I would rather he keep the money for himself and for the boys. Papa is growing old, and he is more likely to need it, especially in the absence of a curate."

Morgan nodded. "It is rather ironical that he keeps insisting on giving you so much," he said sadly. "I must have a profession in order for you to bring that money to the marriage, and yet, if I had obtained a decent position, we would have less use for it."

Judith sighed. "I shall have to speak to him again. Perhaps he will change his mind."

Morgan smiled for the first time. "Your father? Is that likely?"

Judith knew that it was not. Papa was mild enough in the expression of his views, but he did not tend to change them easily. In that way, he and Mr Haddington were similar.

She and her intended were spared further conversation by the complaints of Mrs Guppy, who began fanning herself.

"I cannot tolerate these humours today," she huffed, looking to Mrs Crampton. "Truly, I feel very ill."

"Of course," said the older lady. "We shall get you to your bed, then I shall find one of my tinctures."

"May I help you?" asked Judith, rising, but both ladies waved her away.

"I do well enough with Mrs Crampton," said Mrs Guppy. "You young people ought to enjoy yourselves."

Mrs Haddington, ever the attentive hostess, rang for a maid to help the two ladies to the proper room. Judith overheard her giving specific instructions about broths and medicines that ought to be offered, though Mrs Crampton insisted that she would provide Mrs Guppy with every possible attention and remedy.

As the ladies departed, only Mr Haddington and Morgan expressed concern. The other gentlemen were apparently unmoved. Mr Guppy did not once interrupt his conversation with Mr Lush. Mr Blackmore looked around at the assembled party.

"I am sorry you had to witness such an exhibition," he said, proving himself worse than unmoved.

Mrs Haddington shook her head. "One need never apologize for suffering," she said crisply.

"Truly," the young man said, "this is no more or less than any other lady suffers when she gets to be, er, of a certain age."

Judith's gaze was placid. She shifted very slightly in her seat. "Are we to assume, sir, that pain from causes that are natural and routine is to be discounted entirely?"

Mr Blackmore frowned as he answered. "I suppose it would depend upon the nature of the cause."

Mrs Haddington, for the first time in years, honoured Judith with a most radiant smile.

"Confinement, perhaps," she said. "Or one's courses, each month—"

Judith could not poke fun at the young man, who was turning red, by continuing either of those subjects. Instead, she said, "I wonder if we should reserve treatment for something less common, such as a broken bone, and do nothing for a person with a chill or a fever."

Mr Blackmore did not know quite how to look. And with the other gentlemen engaged in their own conversation, he did not have a rescuer.

"Forgive me," said Mrs Haddington, and Judith briefly thought she might be ready to end the awkwardness. "For a moment, it seemed as if you wished both your mother and your wife to suffer, even to the point of rejecting the mildest and most readily available remedies."

"No, of course not," said Mr Blackmore.

"Then I am sure you ought to praise Mrs Crampton's work just as much as anyone, especially in the coming weeks," said Mrs Haddington.

Judith, who still found herself unable to resist the impulse to rescue the floundering young man, gave an apologetic smile. "I am sure it shall be very useful. It is so easy to catch a chill at this time of year, especially in Derbyshire."

At that, Mrs Haddington actually laughed. "It is no worse than Russia, I am certain," she said.

But as soon as she mentioned that far-off place, the spell was broken. Her expression became less open. Judith remembered the deep resentment she had seen in Mrs Haddington the day that she and Louisa-Margaretta had left for faraway St Petersburg.

"It is better than Russia, yes," said Judith. She should have said that Derbyshire was their home. Only she was no longer certain of that. Her father's position was entirely dependent on the Haddingtons. Mr Haddington, as usual, was so taciturn that he hardly said a word to Judith, but Mrs Haddington's anger had been directed at Judith for years. Ever since Louisa-Margaretta started spending months on end away from her family, in fact. Mrs Haddington had once blamed herself for her daughter's improper entanglements and perpetual spinsterhood, but at some point, she had decided to blame her daughter's dearest friend instead. And though Judith always tried to win back Mrs Haddington's good opinion, she never got on at all. It was a shame, as Mrs Haddington had once thought Judith a very good influence on Louisa-Margaretta.

Judith gave the party a little nod then wandered over to the pianoforte. She had hoped things would end differently, but it appeared that it was still wise for her to avoid Mrs Haddington entirely. And she noticed that Mr Blackmore and Morgan were both making moves to join the gentlemen, who had been relegated to the far corner, so she thought she might as well be with the ladies.

But she could not help gazing at Morgan, wishing that she could will him into finding a perfect opportunity to come speak to her. Somehow, when he was across the room listening to Mr Lush's pronouncements, Judith felt more alone than ever.

7

Mr Barnwell came to breakfast the next morning. For a moment, he was alone with Judith, who was toasting the crumpets.

"I feel that I owe you an explanation," he said, sitting gingerly in one of the family's slender chairs.

Judith could feel her ears burning and knew that her face and neck would also be turning pink.

"You do not," she said. "Though I feel I have not properly congratulated you. We are all very much looking forward to the wedding."

"You will understand, of course," he said, "I have always valued your good opinion, and when I first came to Derbyshire–"

Miriam swept in just then, and though she gave her fiancé a radiant smile, she had words for Judith. "Why did you not tell me Christopher had arrived?"

The sound of his first name on her lips was jarring. Judith realised that she had not even known Mr Barnwell's first name, in spite of his easy manners and the many meals he had taken with her family. She had been sure it was Benjamin or something similar.

"He only just came in," said Judith. "We were speaking of when he first came to Derbyshire."

"Were you?" asked Miriam. "Well, perhaps we might have some time to ourselves now."

"Miriam," said Mr Barnwell helplessly.

"Of course," said Judith.

"And you've burned his crumpet," snapped Miriam. "I shall toast him a better one."

Judith refrained from comment as she left, but the remarks were lodged in her throat as she walked to Wycliff Castle. The road was not at all smooth, but thanks to a spell of sunny weather, some of the snow had melted.

She still flushed when she thought about Mr Barnwell and the offer of marriage he had made to her. That had all come about because she had waited too long to tell her family that she and Morgan were engaged, fearful of what they would say about her decision to marry a Quaker. Though Judith's father had approved when she went to offer her services at a Quaker institution for the mad, recognising in his daughter a moral conviction and desire for action that had informed his own course in life, he felt differently when it came to her leaving the faith entirely.

And though he promised that he was reconciled to her path, the difficulty he was making about Morgan's lack of a profession had put even more of a strain on the atmosphere in the rectory than Judith might have expected.

By the time she reached Wycliff Castle, Judith realised that it was far too early for a polite visit. Even for an intimate friend of the family, it was rather early, as Louisa-Margaretta rarely rose before ten or eleven if she was not forced to. But the footman who received her, Edmund, had long been privy to her desire to see certain members of the household without Mrs Haddington's knowledge. He quickly showed her through to the library, where Morgan met her. It was improper, to be sure, but as a woman of nine and twenty with a longstanding engagement, Judith was sick of standing on ceremony.

They sat together on a settee, as close as they dared. On seeing Morgan, Judith felt some of her resentment melt away, though she was still cross with her sister.

"Miriam has been impossible this morning," Judith said flatly.

Morgan only smiled. "You often describe her that way. And yet, the two of you have managed to live together for two decades or so."

Judith shook her head. She did not like to speak ill of her family, but the past few months had made her feel heartily sick of the requirements of the St Clair household.

"She's very ill-tempered, all because Mr Barnwell once made me an offer! You remember how little interest I took in it," she said. But even raising the subject made her remember how humiliated she had felt, and she hoped Morgan would not reprise the anger that his own response had contained.

Instead, he smiled. "I am ashamed for doubting you. I know you never sought his good opinion. But you'll recall that, at the time, I was an absolute boor."

At last, Judith shared in Morgan's smile. The mild-mannered gentleman before her, who had only ever been accused of rudeness when he demonstrated a little bit too much fellow-feeling with French peasants, must never have been called a boor in his life.

"I could not believe that you felt nothing for him and, moreover, that you had given him no reason for hope," he said. "I should have known that both were true, and yet, my heart got the better of me."

Judith's smile faded, and Morgan hastened to reassure her.

"That does not excuse my behavior," he said. "On the contrary, I could still have chosen to act like a gentleman. And I continue to beg your forgiveness, my dear."

He leaned closer to Judith, and she smiled, though she took care not to touch her fiancé. Their unchaperoned presence in the library would be frowned upon, were it to be discovered, and Judith certainly did not need to add fuel to the fires of gossip with an imprudent embrace.

Though, of course, she was rather tempted.

"But?" she said. "You are surely not going to say that you still harbour some strange dislike of Mr Barnwell?"

"No," he said. "But I will tell you, Miriam's position is much the same. She is in love, which tends to blot out rational thought, and she has made assumptions about your behavior that are ill-founded and unfair."

Judith paused. "For months, I did everything in my power not to be alone with Mr Barnwell. One morning, he comes in while I am toasting the crumpets, and now I am to be pilloried for it?"

Morgan shook his head. "In time, I hope, Miriam will learn that she has secured his affections and that he is a good man. She will not see every conversation as a threat to her future marriage."

Judith shook her head. "Miriam is seeing these shadowy threats everywhere. Ours is the union that is threatened."

Morgan took her hands. "No longer."

Judith knew she ought to pull her hands away, but Morgan's smile and excitement held her captive.

"No longer?" she whispered.

He smiled deeply. "I have invested the last of my money with Mr Lush," he said. "Oh, it will not be immediate, unfortunately. But by next year, Mostiania will bring us both enough wealth to forget about the need for a dowry. If your father still objects to me as a suitor, well, he shall not have the final word."

Judith suppressed her need to cry out in delight. "Oh, my love, that is truly wonderful!"

Morgan took a look at the door then kissed her quickly. Judith instantly flushed, but still she did not pull away.

"When should we expect the money?" she said. "Do you think there is any chance we could marry before then? I don't care what we live on, really."

Morgan shook his head firmly. "I won't marry you if I don't have what we need for a proper household. Imagine, Judith! No coal, in a winter like this one? No, we will wait for the funds to come in."

She smiled, trying to scold him. "Trust you to be sensible," she said as he caressed her hand with his thumb.

Judith was so entranced by the joy in Morgan's face that she did not notice anyone joining them.

"I thought I might find you here," said Louisa-Margaretta, and Judith snatched her hand away. But she knew that guilt as well as joy would be plain enough on her face.

"Yes," Judith said. "I had a rather trying morning with my sister, so I thought you would come for a visit."

"Well, don't let me interrupt," said Louisa-Margaretta.

Morgan stood. "You are hardly interrupting, cousin. Let me give the two of you a moment together, for I have letters to write."

But Louisa-Margaretta would not hear of it.

"Nonsense," she said. "The pair of you ought to enjoy the morning. I shall go and write my own letters."

8

Louisa-Margaretta was determined to avoid Judith and Morgan for the time being. There was nothing more trying than a courting couple, although Louisa-Margaretta did recall that her last engagement had contained no awkwardness or stolen moments of solitude. Mr Solier was handsome, to be sure, and a genius, but he was more besotted with his own musical gifts than with Louisa-Margaretta. Which, perhaps, was why their engagement was destined to end. Louisa-Margaretta was well aware that many love affairs ended in disaster, but she could not stomach the thought of such a union being dull even at the very beginning.

If only Judith and Morgan would make up their minds and marry! Louisa-Margaretta would have married, even without the parental blessing, much earlier. In fact, that had been her plan with Isaac, but when her parents whisked her off to Wycliff Castle, he'd stopped answering her letters. She would gladly have gone with him to Gretna Green, but as it happened, a few hundred miles were all that was needed to break the engagement. Even years later, that still troubled her. Her vanity was permanently wounded. She prided herself on being an excellent judge of character, but in that case, she had been utterly mistaken. And it hurt her heart, because she still preferred Isaac to any other man she had ever known. She might easily find someone else who was interested in her, but falling in love again seemed quite unlikely.

Breakfast was sure to help. It always did. And even if it did not, Louisa-Margaretta was completely incapable of restraining herself when she felt hungry. She marched off to have breakfast with the men, imagining that the ladies would still be abed.

In fact, nobody was eating at all. Papa and Mama would have eaten long ago, and Mrs Guppy and Mrs Blackmore were so fussy about their little illnesses. There was also no trace of Miss Guppy, Miss Blackmore, or Mr Guppy. Young Mr Blackmore was the only person at the table.

He stood immediately. "Good morning, Miss Haddington. I hope this fine day finds you well."

Louisa-Margaretta smiled. Though she was out of spirits, she knew that her white gown and gold necklace became her, setting off the colors in her fiery hair quite nicely.

And indeed, her companion was also dressed in clothing that flattered his coloring. His skin was pale, a marked contrast with his dark hair and eyes. His features were fine and angular, almost like those of a Spaniard, in spite of his fine complexion.

Louisa-Margaretta wondered how Nancy Blackmore, née Guppy, had secured such a handsome man as her husband. The poor woman was quite round, her impending confinement no doubt taking away her bloom, and her features were marred with weariness. Her husband, however, looked perfectly healthy and ridiculously handsome.

"It is indeed a fine day, Mr Blackmore," Louisa-Margaretta said. "Though in winter, I find that there are few in my household who wish to accompany me outdoors. Do you ride?"

He nodded, not taking his eyes off her once. "Of course. Though not as often as I'd like, more recently. Nancy objects to my being far from our home for long, in her, er, condition."

Louisa-Margaretta smirked. "Surely she does not think you will be of much use? What is the very worst that could happen? Mrs Crampton leaves something on a high shelf and you are not there to reach it?"

She felt ashamed as she said it, knowing that Judith would hardly forgive her for making such a vicious remark. But she soon had her reward. Mr Blackmore tossed back his handsome head and laughed.

"I should love to ride while I am here," he said. "But I know nothing of the country, and the hills look quite treacherous."

His meaning was clear, but Louisa-Margaretta took a moment before she answered. First, there was the matter of her plate, and she filled it with every morsel she felt like eating. Though she was well versed in the art of flirtation, she was not going to pretend that she did not need nourishment.

"You have a healthy appetite," said Mr Blackmore approvingly.

Louisa-Margaretta winked. "So I have been told. I do not like to deprive myself. Why should I?"

"Indeed," he said.

Louisa-Margaretta began eating, well aware that she had

not answered Mr Blackmore's question. He stared at her eagerly, not touching his food.

"Well, Miss Haddington? Will you be my guide to the hills of Derbyshire?"

Louisa-Margaretta's heart contracted. She well remembered what had happened the last time boredom and temptation got the better of her. There were a great deal of hills around their home. While her father took a dim view of poaching, her mother hated the practice of employing gamekeepers even more, and Derbyshire had not yet fallen victim to the violent gangs of poachers that raided estates in other parts of the country. So the woods were often quiet, nearly abandoned, and therefore a perfect haven for anyone planning an illicit meeting.

Louisa-Margaretta put her fork down carefully, considering her companion's offer. He was handsome and not devoid of wit. Also, he was cross with his wife, and Louisa-Margaretta must have seemed like quite a fascinating creature by comparison. She could not help but feel thrilled by his attention.

Before, she had always been conscious that married men were quite a risk. After all, if the worst happened, a married man could never be expected to marry her. But she considered that this had its advantages too. One might toy with a married man then act shocked if he attempted to take the flirtation seriously. Louisa-Margaretta must only remember to take care, and she might have a fun and easy Christmas.

"By all means, Mr Blackmore," she cooed. "Only, I must warn you that I am an excellent rider. You shall have to take great pains to keep up."

He grinned broadly then took a bite of eggs dreamily as he gazed into her eyes. After appearing to think it over for a moment, he made a promise.

"We ought to start out together," he said. "If you find that I am too slow for your taste, you have only to show me the way back to the house, and I shan't keep you."

Louisa-Margaretta grinned too. "What chivalry! A perfect gentleman."

"Why of course, Miss Haddington. I aim to please."

9

"We must take greater care, my dear," said Judith, striding down the passageway as quickly as she could manage on her trembling legs. "That was most unpleasant."

Morgan laughed. "Of all the people who could have encountered us, dear Judith, I believe my cousin Louisa-Margaretta is the least likely to make a fuss. Whatever the situation with your family turns out to be, we are soon to be married."

Judith frowned, not sure whether her beloved was alluding to Louisa-Margaretta's transgressions with various men. The trouble was, Louisa-Margaretta was a passionate young woman, and her wild feelings were so often misdirected. She claimed that she would always be happy as a spinster, and yet that had not turned out to be the case. Perhaps if she had been born a man, she could live a life of happy and companionable bachelorhood, spending many hours with any ladies who caught her fancy. But since she was a woman, the restrictions on her were much more severe, and poor Louisa-Margaretta could not help fighting them.

"That is not at all what I meant," she said. "I'm sure Louisa-Margaretta would never give us away, but she was hurt. You must see that."

Morgan nodded. "I suppose so, but what are we to do about it? It shall be worse when we are married."

Judith smiled, thinking of her marriage. "I doubt it. I am always hearing that married women have more time for their friends, not less. At any rate, we ought to at least try to spare her feelings."

Morgan frowned. "We can certainly avoid rooms such as that one, if you think it best."

"I do," said Judith after asking one of the maids to bring her cloak, hat, and muff. "And I think it wise that I go and brave the rectory rather than spending many hours here at Wycliff Castle. Even if Miriam will scold me for burning crumpets."

Morgan's smile was almost invisible, but Judith understood both his mood and his meaning.

"Would you like to take a turn in the garden, then? It has its own barren beauty in winter, as I am sure you are aware."

Judith pulled up the collar of her cloak so that her blush would not be visible to others. The garden was where she and Morgan had spent many hours in the early days of their courtship. With its tall hedges and leafy trees, it was rather secluded in spring, and in spite of the grandeur of Wycliff Castle, there were many spots that were shaded from view. Even in the most innocent days of their acquaintance, Judith recalled how much that solitude and privacy had helped her feel at ease with the intelligent, thoughtful, quietly handsome man who walked beside her.

"I would love to take a turn, Mr Ramsbury," she said formally. "A brief one, on my way home, you understand."

"Of course, Miss St Clair," he said, matching the formal terms of address. Once they were outside, away from any possible listeners, they could say what they liked again.

And indeed, though the hedgerows were but thin collections of branches, Judith could feel her heart opening as they walked in the garden. How she had missed it! Though she suspected she would never feel at home in Wycliff Castle, and she eagerly anticipated her departure from her father's rectory, there was something sacred about Derbyshire. The garden brought the wild peaks and the stern symmetry of the castle into harmony, making each look the better for it.

Morgan's handsome features were pensive, and Judith found herself fighting off an unaccustomed shyness. Though they had been engaged for some time, and sweethearts before then, she had not spent a great deal of time with Morgan in well over a year. She felt that she knew his mind intimately, and yet sometimes, she could hardly speak when they were close together.

Though of course, if she could not speak, she could still walk, and she held tight to his arm as they made their rounds. In spite of what she had said during their departure, she had no need for a quick turn in the garden. Though she disliked winter, she would happily walk with Morgan forever.

"My faith is what has gotten me through the darkest parts of these years," he said, putting an arm around Judith's waist. "And yet, dear Judith, many times, I have wondered whether I ought to give it all up."

"I cannot imagine you as anything but a Quaker, Morgan," she scolded. "And indeed, the tenets of the religion have become woven into my own thinking, as well. What use would it be if you returned to my father's church and I did not follow?"

He laughed, drawing her still closer.

But because the garden was not leafy in winter, they had a little bit of warning. A large, well-clad figure was approaching, and the young couple separated instinctively. Judith took Morgan's arm again but timidly, as if she required some gentleman's arm only to steady her on a cold morning.

"Mr Ramsbury, Miss St Clair," said Mr Guppy, his face already red with cold. Though Mr Haddington was also a stout man, his figure was more imposing. One always got the sense that he was reserved because he chose it, not because he was ineffectual. Mr Guppy, though larger and taller, appeared weak. His eyes darted around, and he took out a handkerchief before putting it away.

His smile, which passed across his face like a fleeting cloud, was nervous. "I had hoped to speak to you, Mr Ramsbury, on a matter of some importance."

Morgan inclined his head politely. "Of course, Mr Guppy. I shall help you if I may. Shall we go inside?"

"No!" was the loud response.

Judith's surprise must have shown on her face, for the gentleman moderated his tone.

"I am sorry. This weather is unpleasant, especially for a lady of delicate constitution," he said. "Miss St Clair, might I ask that you excuse us?"

"Of course," said Judith just as Morgan shook his head.

"You must pardon me," he said. "I am about to walk Miss St Clair to her home. Though, if I may venture a suggestion, as the daughter of a clergyman, she is well-versed in discretion. If there is some private matter that must be resolved, I have no doubt that she would be able to help you far more easily than I would."

Mr Guppy frowned. "Well, if you insist. My wife's cousin plainly does not share my views, so I have not asked any of the Haddingtons. And my son-in-law thinks only of his own amusement, so I am sure he would be of no help either."

Judith thought that a rather cutting view of Mr Blackmore, but she only asked, "And Mr Lush?"

Mr Guppy smiled. "Now, he is a fine fellow, indeed! But I am hoping that he will consider some members of my own family for positions in Mostiania, when the time comes, that is. I shouldn't like to show him that some of us are being made fools of."

Morgan squeezed Judith's arm a bit more tightly, but it was a warning she did not need. She could hardly keep from smiling as she realised that Morgan had not only sensed Mr Guppy's complaint but also had the foresight to ponder Judith's reaction.

He need not have worried. Judith was more than happy to display the discretion and sweetness of temper that had always been expected of a clergyman's eldest daughter.

"That sounds very serious, Mr Guppy. What appears to be the matter?"

When the man took out his handkerchief again but did not speak, she gave him a very small smile. "I can promise you that it shall go no further. Neither Mr Ramsbury nor I approve of gossip, and we may very well have some solution in our power."

Mr Guppy looked about. Judith pursed her lips to keep them from trembling in the cold. Morgan, noticing her discomfort, pressed her arm closer to his side.

"Perhaps we might walk," he suggested. "That will take

us some distance away from any listeners, and we can also speak freely about the matter that is troubling you."

Judith and Mr Guppy agreed to the plan, though the walking itself did not appear to help Mr Guppy. After some moments, he apparently came to a decision and began to speak.

"It's this Mrs Crampton," he said. "She's wormed her way into my wife's confidence, and now she's doing the same with my daughter."

Morgan's steps slowed. "How do you mean, sir?"

Now that Mr Guppy was speaking, he did not appear at all inclined to slow down.

"It started with small things," he said. "My wife was inclined to purchase some of the woman's concoctions. But now she comes to consult, many times a day. My wife sent a considerable gift of money to someone she claims is Mrs Crampton's grown daughter in London, a person none of us has ever met. And she insisted on bringing the old lady all the way here with us, though I insisted many times that we wished to spend Christmas with family."

Morgan's eyebrows went up ever so slightly. Though he was also related to Mrs Haddington, he was no direct relation to the Guppy family.

"As someone who is not a member of your family, sir, I am honoured to be included."

Mr Guppy shook his head. "You're family enough. No, I mean that the Crampton woman ought to be with her own family for Christmas. But instead, she has come all the way to Derbyshire, I know not why."

Judith was puzzled. "She seems to greatly help your wife with her health. Perhaps Mrs Guppy felt that it would be best to have such a person with her, in case she should have a difficult time of it. We have a very different climate here."

"And you have local healers of your own, no doubt," he said. "If Mrs Guppy had wished for some other biddy to take her coin and give her tinctures, she could have gone to such a person here. There was no need to drag an old woman halfway across England."

Judith did not defend the women of her village, as she knew Mr Guppy would not trust any of them. "It does seem like a rather unusual step, but I suppose your wife knows her own mind."

Mr Guppy shook his head darkly. "You don't seem to take my meaning, Miss St Clair. Ever larger sums of money are being leeched away from our family. And to make it worse, Mrs Guppy is spending *my* money on a charlatan."

Judith did not look at her fiancé. They were in dangerous territory indeed.

"Was nothing settled on Mrs Guppy when you married? What a shame that she is spending money that is not her own."

That made Mr Guppy shift on his feet, his large and awkward frame looming over Judith and Morgan.

"She's a Mowbray by birth," he said. "She had a large fortune of her own, same as her cousin did. Or second cousin, I suppose. But we need every shilling for the estate. We cannot see it thrown away on some old woman."

"Indeed," said Judith quietly. "I suppose Mrs Crampton lives on the estate with you, as well?"

Mr Guppy looked away. "My wife offered, of course. I asked her not to, or to just put the woman in one of the old cottages we have. But it all came to naught, as the old lady wouldn't hear of it. She likes staying with a cousin of hers on a farm. Supposed to be nearby, but it is nearly three miles! She can't walk that, though, so my carriage is sent for her night and day."

Morgan nodded. "At least here, at Wycliff Castle, it will be more convenient."

Mr Guppy leaned in, grabbing Morgan's arm. "That's the real difficulty, can't you see? This is the perfect opportunity for her to get her hands on a great deal more money. All in the spirit of Christmas, you see?"

Judith took her arm away from Morgan and walked alongside the two men. Mr Guppy's anger made her acutely uncomfortable, and she wished she could soothe him. But she knew that it would be difficult to get him to stop speaking about that particular subject.

"Perhaps you could tell me what you envision, Mr Guppy," she said. "Though it is possible that Mrs Crampton may spend less time with your wife in future, I hardly imagine she has the funds or the wherewithal to travel all alone at this time of the winter."

"Especially at her age," agreed Morgan.

Judith privately noted that Mrs Crampton had seemed perfectly healthy, much more so than either Mrs Blackmore or Mrs Guppy.

Mr Guppy shook his head. They were approaching the rectory, and Judith knew he would not feel that he could speak freely there. She did not hesitate to press him.

"Would it be enough if we simply observed her closely?" she asked. "If your wife appears poised to spend a great sum, we could be sure to make you aware."

"You could be sure," said Mr Guppy, "to stop her. Miss St Clair, do you not realize that this swindler will stop at nothing?"

Morgan extricated himself from Mr Guppy's grasp and offered his arm to Judith again. "What you say has merit, Mr Guppy. But if Miss St Clair and I are not most delicate in our efforts, we risk offending your wife and forcing her into greater secrecy. That is not the desired outcome, I daresay."

They were quite close to the rectory. Mr Guppy gave an uneasy look at the building, and Judith was reminded of her duty.

"Mr Guppy, it would be my honor to introduce you to my father, my sister, and my younger brothers," she said, though she privately worried that Mr Guppy might be one of those fussy gentlemen who did not like having children underfoot. The rectory, though by far the most spacious accommodation her family had ever occupied, was nonetheless very small compared to what many of the richest families were accustomed to. And Moses, Aaron, and Joseph were quite used to having the run of the place. Their father was gentle, Miriam high-spirited, and Judith more indulgent than even the fondest of mothers. Though the boys were polite enough to visitors, they were not used to sitting silently as grand guests expounded on favoured topics.

"No, thank you, Miss St Clair," he said. "They'll be wondering where I've got to, I daresay. I hate walking on days like this one."

"I would like to come pay my respects to your family, if I may," said Morgan.

"Well, then," said Judith, "I shall rely on seeing you very soon, Mr Guppy."

"Yes," he said. "Don't stay away from Wycliff Castle. You are much needed there. Both of you." And with a small bow, he headed down the lane.

Judith smiled at Morgan, pride and nerves warring within her as they approached her home. She was always glad when Morgan visited them. Her father was so uniformly pleasant, and Morgan's patience with her younger siblings so inexhaustible, that it genuinely seemed as if there were no barriers to her marriage.

That feeling was always temporary, of course. Her father would smile, answer gently, then turn around and refuse his consent the very same day. It was maddening. But at least he did not have the distrust and ill temper that plagued Mr Guppy.

"We may as well go in," Judith told Morgan. "Otherwise, we'll catch our deaths."

He smiled. "This turn about the garden has certainly taken us in an interesting direction. Let us seek the nearest fire."

10

Louisa-Margaretta decided to take Mr Blackmore to the music room. He expressed an interest in hearing her play some of Judith's compositions, although Louisa-Margaretta suspected that he was more interested in proximity to his beautiful new companion than the nuances of composition.

But before she could enter the room, she ran into her mother. Her heart sank. Wycliff Castle was so large that some of the rules about young ladies being chaperoned were necessarily loosely followed. At times, Louisa-Margaretta might encounter a young man when one of her parents was not present, and it was not completely unreasonable that she might not send a servant to fetch her mother immediately.

In that case, however, she could see her mother's eyes flashing. Mama immediately noted the good spirits that were present in both her daughter and the married guest and their clear intention of spending time together in the music room.

"Mr Blackmore, how fortunate that I have found you,"

she said. "Your wife has been feeling most unwell this morning. She has requested your presence."

Mr Blackmore, though he did not look ashamed, was at least aware that argument would be futile. Louisa-Margaretta could not tell whether Mama's reputation had preceded her or, if in less than a day, the young man had got the measure of her character. Mrs Haddington's requests were all orders, and anyone who disobeyed them was most certainly a fool.

"Of course," he said. "You will excuse me."

Louisa-Margaretta looked at the retreating figure of Mr Blackmore, wondering when he might be done with his wife and her tedious complaints.

But Mama seemed able to read her thoughts, for she said, "My dear, it would be lovely if you could help entertain the ladies. I see Miss St Clair has left you."

She touched Louisa-Margaretta's arm, steering her toward the morning room, which was in the opposite direction.

Louisa-Margaretta pulled away, irritated as usual by her mother's refusal to call Judith anything but "Miss St Clair" in conversation.

"She and Cousin Morgan went for a walk, I believe," said Louisa-Margaretta. "Though how Judith is faring in this cold, I cannot imagine."

Mama gave a little sigh of sympathy and patted Louisa-Margaretta's shoulder. "There, now. Every young lady gets a little bit silly when there is a wedding to come. And we haven't a hope of changing either party's mind, though I have spoken to Cousin Morgan about my reservations."

Louisa-Margaretta stopped in the middle of the passageway. "Oh, Mama, surely not!"

Her mother only smiled. "Indeed I have, my dear. Since his own mother is not living, I could hardly do otherwise."

Louisa-Margaretta gave a most unladylike snort. "Well, I very well hope he ignored you. What objections to Judith herself could you possibly have, other than the fact that she has taken my side at every turn!"

Her mother frowned. "It is not quite taking your side, dear, if she encourages you in all sorts of foolish pursuits. That place in Essex, where you did not belong at all, and then to go to Russia! And not only the circumstances, but the *company*—"

"It was the making of me," said Louisa-Margaretta sternly. Indeed, she wondered if she could go quite as far as that. Even after the strange places she had been with Judith, she still had a knack for finding trouble wherever she was. Their last destination had "only" been London, but Louisa-Margaretta had become entangled in the murder of a man who had once meant a great deal to her. She ended the whole thing with a broken engagement and a promise to return to Derbyshire and lick her wounds. One could hardly say that she was "much improved" by her experiences. But without them, she knew she would still be the same person who'd originally come to Wycliff Castle. In those days, she had thought only of herself and Isaac and known nothing at all of the world. If she was not perfectly wise, at least she was more aware and much more observant.

"As I said," Mama went on, "it is all to be forgot, for they shall marry with or without my blessing. We will congratulate your cousin Morgan, and that will be the end of it."

Louisa-Margaretta paused. "I am not sure, Mama. Mr St Clair keeps nothing from you, so I am sure he has told you that he somehow amassed a small fortune for Judith's dowry. And that he is refusing to give it to her unless Cousin Morgan proves himself by finding a profession."

Mama would not allow the conversation to continue. In fact, she turned rather pink, which was unusual. "Mr St Clair ought not to make any such demands on Cousin Morgan." Then, in a contradiction, she added, "And this is none of our business, I am sure. Come, Louisa-Margaretta, all the ladies are here. And our gathering would be enlivened by your company."

11

As soon as she entered the room, Louisa-Margaretta saw that the gathering absolutely needed to be enlivened.

Mrs Guppy's face was pink, and though the day had only grown colder, she was standing by an open window, breathing heavily. Mrs Crampton seemed to be supporting her, murmuring words of encouragement. Miss Blackmore smiled when Louisa-Margaretta entered, but Miss Guppy scowled.

"I understand you are political, Miss Haddington," said Miss Blackmore. "I've been hearing about your time in Russia."

"Well, you do not hear anything accurate," said Louisa-Margaretta, wishing she could share some of the stories with Miss Blackmore but knowing that she had to pretend her trip was rather frivolous. "I know little of politics."

"Surely," said Miss Blackmore, "thanks to your brothers, you must know a bit more than I do."

"My brother Augustus could probably tell me a great deal, if he bothered to write," mused Louisa-Margaretta.

"And Sherborne has been rather frantic, complaining of prices dropping."

Miss Blackmore frowned. "He is in business with your father, then?"

"Yes," said Louisa-Margaretta, "in Manchester for the moment, though he prefers London. My brother Percival put something about the Apothecaries Act in his last letter, though why he thinks it would interest me, I cannot say."

Miss Guppy gave a little smile. "Papa loved the Apothecaries Act. And Mama hates it. You should raise the subject at our next meal. We'll see how it divides the table."

"Jessie," said Miss Blackmore with a grin. "It would be terrible to provoke them in that manner."

"Your parents have nothing to do with the business of providing medicines, surely," said Louisa-Margaretta. "A row would be amusing, of course, but why are they so interested in all this? I still don't even understand what has changed."

Miss Blackmore gave Miss Guppy a warning look, but the usually taciturn young woman moved closer, her grin rather wicked.

"The act says that only a person with proper training ought to be able to distribute medicines," she said. "Any person who now distributes any remedy, if he *or she* does not have the right credentials, is officially considered a fraud."

"Jessie—"

"As well as unofficially."

For the first time, Miss Blackmore looked genuinely worried. Louisa-Margaretta saw that she was glancing at the large chair where Mrs Guppy was sitting, fanning herself languidly, while Mrs Crampton murmured to her.

"Is Mrs Crampton not permitted to give anyone her medicines, then?" Louisa-Margaretta asked Miss Guppy.

"Well," said Miss Guppy, "it entirely depends on the nature of the service, as well as the payment received."

Miss Blackmore frowned. "You must understand, one woman befriending another, sharing the sort of remedies that we have always used... well, that ought not to be considered *medicine*, precisely."

"Even though it's a good bit more effective than any of the medicines those physicians give us," grumbled Jessie. "They did almost nothing for Mama."

Louisa-Margaretta, who had always regarded illness as weakness, privately agreed. The most competent physicians she had ever known were those who acknowledged the role of informal remedies as well as scientific ones, though she had required a trained physician to help her once, when she was poisoned. She wondered if an old charlatan like Mrs Crampton would have been of much use under those circumstances or if she would have given Louisa-Margaretta some useless advice and remained unaware of the root cause.

"How long has Mrs Crampton been with your family?" asked Louisa-Margaretta.

Miss Guppy shot Miss Blackmore a mysterious look but was saved from answering by a disturbance.

A maid came rushing in. Louisa-Margaretta recognized Harriet, who was normally rather steady, breathing heavily.

"If you please, ma'am." She addressed her mistress but allowed her remarks to be heard by the whole room. "It's Mrs Blackmore. She is unwell, and she hopes that someone might attend her."

"I shall send for the doctor," said Mrs Haddington. "And we shall go to her presently, of course."

"My little girl!" said Mrs Guppy. Though her face was red, all thoughts of her own trouble were plainly forgotten.

Miss Guppy, for the first time, looked worried rather than peevish. Miss Blackmore, ever encouraging, went to the other girl and took her hand. "You needn't worry, Jessie," she said in a low voice. "It's all to be expected. Mrs Crampton will know what to do."

Mrs Crampton, Louisa-Margaretta noticed, was not hastening to the door.

"She'll be having pains again," she said. "Someone must play and sing to her. She'll forget them soon enough. It's not her time."

"It will be early," said Mrs Guppy, but Mrs Crampton soothed her.

"Hush, then."

The old woman looked about the room. "Miss Haddington? Perhaps you could arrange for an instrument and someone to play it. Yourself?"

Louisa-Margaretta dismissed that notion immediately. "I shall send someone to move an instrument, yes. And I can ask Miss St Clair to play it. I know very few tunes, but she will play much better."

That was a lie. Louisa-Margaretta, when she was in the right sort of mood, could play for a great length of time. But she could not imagine herself sitting in the room with Mrs Blackmore, a young woman large with child, listening to constant moans and complaints. The thought alone disgusted her. No, she would go find Judith, who would no doubt happily spend a whole afternoon keeping the invalid entertained.

12

Judith and Morgan spent the walk to Wycliff Castle discussing the St Clair family. But that time, it was not Miriam and Mr Barnwell who occupied their conversation. The engaged pair had been off taking a walk around the village with plans to call on the Chandlers before Mr Barnwell returned to some of his clerical duties. It was Judith's brothers who occupied their conversation, particularly Joseph, the youngest.

"He is hardly eating," said Judith. "I fear something has upset him."

Morgan was more skeptical. "He seems to have enough energy to torment his brothers. The way he was hitting Moses!"

Judith gave a wry laugh. "Yes, Moses and Aaron do not always have time for him, but they have never used such violence. Ordinary scuffles, to be sure, but not hitting hard enough to bruise or draw blood. Papa is horrified."

"Well might he be," said Morgan. "Your father is a peaceful man. I do not understand how Joseph has come to have such a violent temper."

Judith sighed. "I have tried to ask Joseph himself a dozen times. All I wish for him to tell me is what provokes him, why he has become both withdrawn and angry. Between denying that there is any trouble and running away from me, he never chooses to answer."

Morgan sighed. "One can tell him not to hit his brothers."

Judith felt herself growing angry. Joseph's behavior had been worsening since Michaelmas, and Morgan clearly had no sense of all of the avenues she had gone down in attempting to correct him.

"If I give him the mildest rebuke, he begins sobbing and will not speak," she said. "If I even remind him that he is not to lay hands on his brothers, he may cry and refuse to play with either of them."

"And yet, each time he does join in their games, it appears that he intends to hurt both of them," said Morgan. "But I suppose children do not think of it in such a way."

Judith sighed. She knew that she should not be vexed with Morgan for his lack of understanding, but he did not appear to appreciate the gravity of Joseph's disquiet.

"I have never seen him like this," she said quietly. "Not even after Mama died. Well, that was a horrible time, to be sure. But he was so young and so gentle."

Morgan nodded. "Boys are taught to strike others and never to cry. I suppose that is part of the trouble."

Judith nodded, though such was not the case in her family. "What were you taught?" she asked carefully. She rarely talked to Morgan about his childhood, but it seemed important to establish his ideas on such matters before they dealt with children of their own. Such a prospect had always seemed rather remote to Judith, but if they were to marry soon, she might find herself sharing Mrs Nancy Blackmore's pitiable condition before too long.

Morgan gave a wry smile. "I was taught that for even a minor transgression, I would be hit or kicked. And so, I suppose, I learned how to hit others. It is one of the things that first drew me to the Quakers. Even now, you know, they have schools for children where violent methods are never used."

Judith nodded fiercely. "That is so important! Papa was never willing to send any of us away to school for that reason. Although, in my case and Miriam's, I think he was also worried that we would learn little of any substance."

"Surely the two of you would learn at any institution," protested Morgan, but Judith shook her head.

"Many of the schools teach deportment and the basics of languages, but they are rather adamantly against independent thought," she said. "Papa was concerned that we would be overly interested in dancing and forget everything we knew of theology. Though I do think it would have been better for Miriam to make more friends. Until she met the Chandlers, she was quite alone in Derbyshire, and that was very hard on her."

He drew her toward him, coming perilously close to what would be considered indecent behavior.

"I count myself fortunate that you are brilliant, Judith, and that no school has been able to tarnish your mind or your character," he said, and she smiled without looking at him.

At that moment, Louisa-Margaretta came marching out of the house, and Judith once again pulled away from her fiancé too late. How infrequent their embraces had been, and yet that was the second one that Louisa-Margaretta had interrupted! If she had not been feeling alone and hurt before, she certainly would be then.

Louisa-Margaretta's manner was brusque, of course. Judith knew her friend well enough to know that there would be no direct discussion of wounded pride or hurt feelings.

"Mrs Blackmore is carrying on," Louisa-Margaretta said. "She requested that an instrument be moved to her room and a musician be sent to play it! Imagine such a thing."

"Is it to do with the baby?" asked Judith, but Louisa-Margaretta shook her head.

"Their Mrs Crampton said it is not her time, though how she has any idea, I do not know. Mama has sent for the doctor, and I was sent to fetch you."

"Me?" asked Judith. She had attended women in such circumstances, of course. Oftentimes, the curate's wife was one of the first women to arrive, and as a widower, Mr St Clair was often forced to send Judith.

"Yes," said Louisa-Margaretta firmly. "I'm certainly not going to go in there and rustle about, trying to find a tune that the little princess will enjoy. In fact, as soon as I am dressed, I shall go out riding."

It did not escape Judith's notice that Louisa-Margaretta did not invite her cousin Morgan to join her.

"Very well," she said, hesitating. "I suppose I shall go to her bedroom and see what I can manage."

"That's very good of you," said Louisa-Margaretta before striding back into the castle without bothering to wait for either Judith or Morgan.

13

When Judith arrived in the room, fearful not only of death but also of blood and suffering, Mrs Blackmore had been reduced to whimpers. Mrs Crampton rose from her bedside.

"It is good of you to come," she said gently. "There's nothing for it! Our Nancy needs a tincture with hot milk and a little bit of music. She'll soon be well."

Judith sat at the instrument, feeling the oddity of its placement, and ran through some of J. S. Bach's compositions. They came easily to her fingertips, as she had once spent a great deal of time using them to calm a different lady's nerves. And though she might be loath to admit it, Judith found them soothing as well. The twin questions of her dowry and Joseph's temper, which had been tormenting her for some time, fell away under her methodical playing. And after a while, she noticed that Mrs Blackmore had gone quieter. The girl's face, scared and innocent on the pillows, relaxed into a visage that was puffy yet pretty. Judith paused, and Mrs Blackmore applauded tentatively.

"Do continue, if you would, Miss St Clair," said young Mrs Blackmore.

"There's a good girl," said Mrs Crampton. "There's nothing so helpful as music."

"Where is Mama?" asked Mrs Blackmore.

Mrs Crampton gave a little chuckle. "I sent her away. She was moaning more than you were, my dear! I couldn't have her distressing you."

Mrs Blackmore sighed loudly. "She wants to help, but everything she does hinders us. She brought us all the way here to Derbyshire. I only wanted to be home."

"Which home?" asked Judith, and the young woman started.

"Pardon?"

Judith shook her head. "I'm so sorry. I only wondered. Of course Derbyshire is not your home. Would you prefer to be in your mother's house or by your own hearth?"

Mrs Blackmore sighed, resting her hands on her large belly. "Oh, I suppose my own home. But Mama could see well enough that I was not happy there."

Judith began to play again, though her stomach was lurching. She always assumed that, loving Morgan as she did, marriage would be a perfect step for them. But she could easily imagine feeling lonely and overwhelmed as a new wife. She had always lived with a great many other people, either siblings or friends, and it would be odd for her to be alone. Well, alone apart from a new husband.

"I am sure it is strange," she murmured.

A maid came in with the hot milk, and Mrs Crampton carefully mixed one of her tinctures into it, counting out the drops with a surprisingly steady hand. Only when the maid had left and Mrs Blackmore had taken a few delicate sips did she continue speaking.

"It was well enough when we were first married," Mrs Blackmore said. "But my condition has made life very difficult. In the early days, I was either very ill or ready to yell at my husband, which was most unbecoming."

"He ought to hear a little yelling," murmured Mrs Crampton. "Men yell at each other often enough. In fun, half the time, or so they claim."

Mrs Blackmore, overcome, set down her cup of milk. A tear rolled down her cheek. Mrs Crampton, without being asked, produced a clean handkerchief. Judith, thanks to her expert knowledge of J. S. Bach's music, was able to watch the entire exchange without pausing in her playing. But she began to feel ashamed, so she looked down at the keys.

"You must not blame my mother, Miss St Clair," said Mrs Blackmore. "She only wished to help Reuben and me."

"Of course," said Judith. "Any mother would wish to help her child. And her grandchild."

Mrs Crampton looked at Judith approvingly. "Indeed. She wished to help her daughter, bless her. As to her son-in-law, I'm not sure there were any motives there. Perhaps she thought that seeing the fine example set by Mr Haddington would give him a sense of duty to his wife and child."

It was Judith's turn to be impressed. As far as she could tell, Mrs Crampton was quite sincere in her praise for the man of the house, and Judith was surprised that she had not thought Mr Haddington rather dull. Indeed, for quite a time, Judith had thought her friend's father was a silly man, particularly because he seemed to get flustered every time he had to say two words to any of the St Clairs. But she had come to appreciate both his heart and his intellect, and she wondered how Mrs Crampton had divined his true character so easily.

Even Judith had to admit it was possible that Mr Guppy

was right in his assumptions about the old woman. Presumably, he, too, wanted the best for his child, and Judith was not at all sure it had been wise to give Mrs Blackmore a tincture before the doctor arrived. Mrs Crampton seemed like a perfect caregiver for the distressed girl, but then, if she had a mercenary aim, it was only natural that she should be solicitous. Judith decided to continue observing both.

"I'm feeling much better," said Mrs Blackmore. "Miss St Clair, if you would be so good, you may let my mother know. I can only really tolerate her fussing after the crisis passes, you see."

Judith smiled. "I am glad to hear it. I'll fetch her now."

As she made her way to the morning room, where she suspected she would still find most of the ladies, Judith reflected on her mission. She was supposed to report any large promises of money to Mr Guppy, but she was not sure whether to do so. If he held most of the purse strings, it hardly mattered if Mrs Guppy was generous with her pocket money. But Mrs Crampton, if she was a charlatan, was clearly highly skilled. And that meant that the Haddingtons, as one of the wealthiest families in England, would make an excellent target.

Judith stopped short. That might well be the woman's aim! The Guppy family had money, to be sure, but they presumably were not in quite the same echelon as the Haddingtons. And if Mrs Crampton had persuaded Mrs Guppy to travel to Derbyshire in the middle of winter, perhaps she had serious designs on the family. Though none of the Haddingtons were fools, they were still human, and Judith did not at all doubt that all of them were seeking comfort of some kind.

14

When Judith finally found Louisa-Margaretta, the latter was in her bedchamber, dressing for a ride.

"I don't know where Cousin Morgan is, Judith," she said shortly. "And I am certainly the wrong person to ask."

"I had hoped to speak with you, not with Morgan," said Judith evenly, but Louisa-Margaretta only adjusted her riding habit.

"I have got to get some new clothes next time we go to London," she said. "I have already gone through half of my trousseau, so I suppose it's rather good that I broke the engagement. I daresay the tedium of shopping is worth it if it means I do not have to endure such ancient styles."

"Not quite as ancient as the brown riding habit," said Judith. "May I wear it?"

Louisa-Margaretta shrugged. "I am sure there are many other things you would rather do than ride with me. Mr Blackmore could not join me this time, but he will soon, so I have to keep up my customary pace."

"Very well," said Judith. "But I only need to speak with you for a few moments."

"You can do that here," said Louisa-Margaretta.

One of the newer housemaids was helping her, and Judith decided it would be more effective for her to address the young woman instead. "Could you bring me Miss Haddington's brown riding habit? She seldom uses it, and it fits me fairly well."

"Very good, miss."

They said nothing while Judith dressed for the excursion. Louisa-Margaretta sighed, pacing the floor as she waited, and she did not say a word to Judith as they went out into the yard. It was only when they were off, on horses that had been groomed perfectly, that she deigned to speak once again.

"You need not accompany me out of pity," said Louisa-Margaretta. "Though I no longer have a fiancé of my own, I daresay I can pass one solitary afternoon."

Judith fought the urge to remind Louisa-Margaretta that she had certainly not planned to pass the afternoon alone. Most likely, she had invited the handsome Mr Blackmore, but he was otherwise engaged.

She said nothing of that, however. Judith knew her friend well enough to realize that if she said to go east, Louisa-Margaretta would urge her horse into a westward gallop. If she did not express any disapproval of Louisa-Margaretta's interest in Mrs Blackmore's husband, perhaps the flames of desire would die out on their own.

"Spending an afternoon with you is always a pleasure," said Judith. When her friend made no response, she said, "Well, almost always."

Louisa-Margaretta blinked in surprise. "Your sister must be more beastly than I am for you to say such things."

Judith shook her head. "I hardly know what to make of Miriam, I confess. But that is not why I wished to speak with you."

"We could have spoken in Wycliff Castle," said Louisa-Margaretta. "You're already shivering."

Judith noticed that it was true. She wished that she could transform the countryside into a leafy spring instead of those frigid days before Christmas. It made her long for Russia, with its warm interiors and short distances. Though the empire itself was vast, she and Louisa-Margaretta had been in St Petersburg, so the distance from one drawing room fire to the next was never a long one.

"Remember the canals of St Petersburg?" she asked.

"Ha!" said Louisa-Margaretta. "Yes, they were deadly. Surely you haven't forgotten what happened to the prince? Though, of course, that was hardly an accident."

Judith's heart sank. She had been recalling the beauty of the canals, frozen over, filled in with snow that had been dumped from the streets and branches, the candlelight of dozens of homes illuminating that lovely feature.

But Louisa-Margaretta had a better memory for the sinister, and it reminded Judith that she had to tell her friend all her worries. Out of habit, she looked into the cold woods around them, but she saw nobody.

"Louisa-Margaretta," she said, "is the Guppy family very rich? Or the Blackmore family?"

Louisa-Margaretta rolled her eyes. "They have nobody of marriageable age, unless you count the young ladies. If your brothers wait a decade or so, one of them may snag Miss Guppy. But Miss Blackmore seems to delight in spurning all her suitors, so something tells me she will not marry until she's had her fun."

Judith sighed. "I do not ask for that reason, of course.

But you must believe that I have my own reason for wishing to know."

Louisa-Margaretta urged her horse into a trot, and Judith followed reluctantly. She was glad to see the serene expression that Louisa-Margaretta's face always took on when she was riding, hunting, or otherwise engaged in a challenge. It was something that Judith had rarely seen since their return from Russia. And all of the trouble in London, both with the murder of a scoundrel and the wild accusations that followed, had been quite a challenge for Louisa-Margaretta.

Judith drew a breath, hoping she had not had a sinful thought of wishing for someone's death. For Louisa-Margaretta was never happy that another person had died. But her reckless intelligence always came to the fore when she and Judith looked for a culprit, and she had no such animation in a drawing room.

"The Guppy family has enough money," said Louisa-Margaretta. "Mr Guppy himself has five thousand a year, I believe. The Blackmores have less, which was one reason Mr Blackmore married where he did, in case you had been wondering."

"Indeed not," said Judith, knowing that she spoke with too much vehemence. "I should not presume to speculate about any young person's reason for marrying."

Louisa-Margaretta's voice was merry. "Oh, how the ladies of Almack's would love you, Judith! Should not presume to speculate, indeed. When a young lady of considerable fortune marries a young man in need of money, you are the only young woman in England who does not engage in speculation."

"Very well," said Judith stiffly.

Louisa-Margaretta, her smile suffusing her whole being,

breathed in the cool air. "What was your reason for asking, then?"

Judith frowned. "An idea occurred to me, Louisa-Margaretta, but you must promise me not to repeat it."

"I shall make no promise of the kind. However, you know that I can keep a secret almost as well as you can."

"Yes," said Judith, still unwilling to slander a woman who had appeared to be helpful and kind. However, though she did not wish to see it, there was something canny about Mrs Crampton. Judith had known more than one woman who was not quite what she made out, and Mrs Crampton had a watchfulness common to people who lied habitually. It was the one reason that Judith had not been entirely averse to Mr Guppy's suggestion. Though he might dismiss Mrs Crampton's abilities, he might also have happened upon something true. As Judith's aunt Leah was fond of saying, a broken clock was right twice a day.

"Come, Judith," said Louisa-Margaretta. "If you do not tell me, I shall get it out of someone. Does Cousin Morgan know?"

That would be worse. "Yes," said Judith quickly. "He was with me when Mr Guppy—er—made his appeal. He wants the two of us to help him with something rather peculiar."

Louisa-Margaretta grinned. "Probably asked you to find a husband for that daughter of his. Miss Guppy's temper is more likely to be heightened by matrimony than cured by it. You can tell him that."

"No," said Judith. "He wished for us to, well, look into Mrs Crampton's origins. And her aims, I believe. He seems to feel that she is out to swindle his family."

"She's doing a terrible job of keeping it secret, then. She is quite open about her little remedies, and what harm is it, really, if Mrs Guppy is paying her for them?"

"It is a bit odd for Mrs Crampton to travel with the Guppy family," said Judith. "Particularly to travel, well, here."

"Yes, Derbyshire is rather horrid this time of year," said Louisa-Margaretta. "Mama could be kind and warn all the visitors about it, but she is so desperate for company, she keeps inviting them. If anyone has the ability to swindle others, it is she."

"No," said Judith. "I don't wish to speak ill of Mrs Crampton, but is it possible she is after your own family's money?"

Judith blushed. It was awkward, at times, speaking to Louisa-Margaretta about money when her family had such a vast fortune. Though, to be fair, Louisa-Margaretta wouldn't get any piece of that fortune until she married.

"Oh, Judith." She sighed. "Even if she did swindle my parents, I daresay we could afford it. Was that the only thing?"

Judith hesitated. "About your, well, your friend. Mr Isaac Rodrigo—"

"No," said Louisa-Margaretta. "That is quite enough."

Judith could hear the flare of her friend's temper. She knew that Louisa-Margaretta had never really given up her beloved Isaac, at least, not in the deepest part of her heart. Judith also knew that there was little she could personally do to convince Louisa-Margaretta to speak of it.

And indeed, in the next moment, she was banished.

15

"You may go, Judith," Louisa-Margaretta said. "I suppose you will want to see my cousin before you go?"

Judith frowned. "No, I should not like to overstay my welcome. But take care. I feel that your guests are causing some difficulties here, and I do not feel easy about what I have seen."

Louisa-Margaretta's laugh was short. "I can manage the guests. And I shall make sure neither of my parents falls prey to an unscrupulous granny, Judith."

She was amused to see Judith shudder at the thought, rushing back to the rectory, likely with all sorts of guilt over making such a scandalous insinuation.

There would be no such guilt for Louisa-Margaretta. Where there was smoke, she felt sure that she would find fire. And though she very much hoped that her parents would not believe any of Mrs Crampton's words, Louisa-Margaretta recalled that her mother had once said that Mrs Guppy had "a very good head on her shoulders." Well, if a woman of sense and good breeding could fall for such a scheme, perhaps Louisa-Margaretta ought to take a little more care. Though her parents would probably not spend enough on Mrs Crampton's remedies to ruin them, still, it might prove humiliating to be so taken in.

After careful inquiries, she learned that her father was entertaining one of the visitors in his study, and she worried that the old woman had already moved in for the kill. Fortunately, the visitor in question was only Mr Lush, so Louisa-Margaretta took her time as she found the best way to observe them.

Fortunately, she was not searching for long. It was quite possible to hear nearly everything that was said between the two men from an adjoining room. There had once been a door in between the rooms, and though her father had put a desk in front of it, the fact remained that one could hear rather well at that particular location. There was even the narrowest crack, so Louisa-Margaretta could see as well as hear.

When she neared the door, she saw that her father had put a hand up to his brow, as he occasionally did during times of great distress.

"Can you be trusted to keep this quiet? I wonder," her father said.

Louisa-Margaretta raised her eyebrows. Mr Lush, she had noted, loved to talk. She would never have trusted him with a secret of hers. But perhaps her father was not familiar with his type.

"My business has been greatly troubled of late," Papa said. "There has been difficulty with the workers as well as the machinery, and I am very worried about what is to come."

"Then this is the perfect time," said Mr Lush. "You need

to put your money where it will work for you, sir, rather than leaving it all in a difficult business."

Louisa-Margaretta heard a sharp bark of laughter from her father.

"It is all difficult, I 'spose," he said.

Louisa-Margaretta winced as she heard her father's humble origins make their way into his manner of speaking. Typically, he was very careful about his diction, but in that conversation, he had begun to sound like a poor man from Manchester once more.

"Everything has a cost," he said.

Mr Lush nodded vigorously and took a great gulp of the wine that his host had poured for him.

"Of course," he said. "And I do not pretend that voyaging to the land of milk and honey is easy. Far from it, the passage itself is difficult and lengthy! But the worth, my dear man! You could set all your children up for the future."

"They all are set up," her father said shortly. "Well, except for my daughter, but one needn't worry about her."

Mr Lush gave a large grin. "Of course not! With your daughter's wit and beauty, she is not going to last long in the London ballrooms."

Louisa-Margaretta rolled her eyes. She had already been in and out of such ballrooms for a decade, and if she could find a way to avoid setting foot in them in future, she certainly would. Most of the men and women there seemed like children to her. It would, however, be easy enough to find a fortune hunter to marry her, no matter what her age.

"Speak no more of Miss Haddington," her father said, formality creeping back into his diction as he became offended. "This is a business question."

"Of course," said Mr Lush, and Louisa-Margaretta nearly stamped her foot. That was to be the extent of her role in the conversation, then! She did not cause any degree of worry, according to her father, and Mr Lush would mindlessly flatter without even informing himself about Louisa-Margaretta's age or interest in marriage. Both men were far more interested in business.

"As I said, my business is in dire straits at the moment," said Mr Haddington. "I don't think I can spare a single farthing."

"Oh, sir," said Mr Lush. "Surely one farthing is as nothing to a great man such as yourself! I am quite sure you could come up with a princely sum for my endeavors in spite of whatever little difficulties trouble your business. I can see that you have spared no expense in entertaining, and while I am thankful, I must believe that you have some optimism yet about your prospects."

Mr Haddington shook his head, gloom etched in every one of his features. "Indeed not. I would be a fool if I thought so."

Louisa-Margaretta bit her lip. Her father had said nothing to her about such difficulties! It was true, they rarely spoke of his business, but if they were hard up for money, surely she and her mother ought to know. Only last month, she had begged him for a new horse, and he had obliged by procuring not one but two beautiful mares.

"I can spare five hundred pounds," he said. "It may ruin me, but you are a wise man, Mr Lush. I cannot miss such an opportunity."

With that, Mr Lush gained even greater animation, embracing his host and reassuring him of his wisdom. "That is all you will need, sir. Before long, you may wish to make it a thousand pounds, but truly, that is all you ought to need. You will see it blossom and grow many times over!"

"Indeed," said Mr Haddington. "I will get it for you straightaway."

"Yes, yes," said Mr Lush. "A wise decision, sir!"

Louisa-Margaretta stepped back from the door, struck by the exchange. She was disturbed by Judith's assertion. If her father was indeed experiencing financial difficulties, it was all the more dangerous for Mrs Crampton to stay with them. Her father could not turn down anyone he thought was good-hearted, apparently. He had given in to Mr Lush's entreaties almost immediately, and at least that man was promising a return on the investment. Mrs Crampton would simply ask for funds and promise to keep the Haddington family in tinctures or some such thing.

Louisa-Margaretta knew that she ought to go to her mother. The formidable Mrs Haddington was the only person living who truly had the upper hand with Wycliff Castle, and she did not hesitate to use it either. But extricating Mama from the circle of sick women she had gathered around her would not be easy.

16

The afternoon was difficult, as Mrs Haddington loved a sickroom. She was determined to lavish every possible attention on the invalids, and it was not until they all sat down to dine that Louisa-Margaretta saw an opportunity.

She would have to get through the meal first, though. And while she was tolerably close to Mr Blackmore, his sister was in between them.

Louisa-Margaretta got through her soup quickly, trying to think of a way of flattering Jessie Guppy out of her terrible mood. There were techniques she had learned long ago that worked tolerably well with madwomen. She decided to employ one of those after Miss Guppy batted away Louisa-Margaretta's first attempts at conversation.

"I know little about Christmases in the Guppy family," she said merrily. "Are there any particular games you are eager for us to include?"

"Your mother did not seem very enamoured of Christmas games," Mr Blackmore broke in with a charming smile. "Though I love all of them, of course. And she said she absolutely would not allow the tradition of a mistletoe ball in Wycliff Castle."

He looked so very sad that Louisa-Margaretta laughed. "Why, yes, Mama will insist on bringing out a 'praying ball.' I can assure you we are the only family in England who has one. It is expected that one stand underneath and offer up a prayer. Only a true zealot could fall in love beneath such an abomination."

Her eyes twinkled as she said it. Cousin Morgan, across the table, blushed and looked away. Louisa-Margaretta recalled that the inaugural year of the "praying ball" was the season when Judith and Cousin Morgan fell in love. And indeed, she often saw them in earnest prayer and conversation beneath that very spot. Perhaps, for the two shy and God-fearing individuals, a prayer ball was a better matchmaker than the traditional "kissing ball" would have been.

But unencumbered by guilt, Louisa-Margaretta continued her conversation with the Guppy family. "Is there a certain game we ought to play first, Miss Guppy?" she asked, mindful of her mother's eyes from the end of the table. Mama would be upset if she felt that Louisa-Margaretta was neglecting the taciturn Jessie Guppy, though making polite conversation with a stone monument might have been easier.

Miss Guppy had hardly touched her food. She sighed. "I find the games tedious. But you play well, Louisa-Margaretta. Perhaps you and your friend Miss St Clair could entertain us with your music."

Louisa-Margaretta paused in surprise, on the verge of taking another spoonful of soup but impressed with the answer. "I like writing new words to the carols. Will that trouble you?"

Miss Guppy looked curious rather than cross. "No, I

don't believe so. Perhaps you will play some of your compositions for us tomorrow?"

Louisa-Margaretta nodded. She did not like to be confined indoors, but when she and Judith were creating new musical compositions, she was almost as happy as when she went hunting. It was one of the reasons she thought she might like to be an opera composer's wife, that was, until the experience of being engaged to Mr Solier changed her mind.

"Perhaps I might add some words of my own," mused Miss Guppy.

Louisa-Margaretta was amazed that she had captured the young lady's attention, but before she could respond, she heard a long gasp from Miss Blackmore.

"How horrid," the young lady was saying to Miss Haddington.

Judith's mother leaned in closer. "Quite. And they say it is not the first bank that has failed in this area."

"Banks are failing all over the country," said Mr Blackmore. "That's why they aren't good places to put a fortune."

Mr Haddington leaned back, his eyebrows raised. "Where, then?"

Mr Lush should have been happy, thought Louisa-Margaretta. That was the perfect opening for him to go on about his little South American project again. But instead, he agreed with Mr Blackmore, his expression grim.

"I cannot tell you how much I agree with your opinion," he said. "That a bank can close and not pay out any of the funds? It's disgraceful."

Mr Guppy blinked at both of them. "I hope you're not part of those radicals who say we shouldn't have banks. Or worse, those men who seem to think that everyone should be paid for doing nothing at all!"

"What solution would you propose, Mr Guppy?" asked Judith.

Louisa-Margaretta smiled. Of the people at the table, only she knew that Judith was challenging the man. The question was asked with such respect, such seeming sweetness, that the poor man would be sure that the young lady was asking for his advice.

It occurred to her that Cousin Morgan probably also knew Judith's conversational gambits, and that dampened her spirits.

"I do not propose that anything be done about it," said Mr Guppy. "A gentleman oughtn't to keep his money in only one bank, that's all."

"And a lady?" asked Miss Blackmore, without Judith's sweetness.

"The same," said Mr Guppy. "If she has a man with some expertise advising her, of course."

Cousin Morgan took up the supposedly radical side of the argument. "If a system is working poorly for a large part of the populace, one cannot escape the conclusion that something is at issue with the system itself. The banks that succeed bring in enormous profits for their backers, whereas those that fail do not force the responsible parties to face any consequences."

"So they ought to be hanged, then?" asked Mr Guppy. "Odd to hear a fellow like you say that. I always thought the Quakers didn't like hanging."

Cousin Morgan turned red with the teasing. "Certainly, that is not the only possible consequence—"

"Oh, something mild," said Mr Blackmore, joining in with his father-in-law. "Well, I am sure that a mere reprimand would have a deterrent effect."

The servants, who had been removing dishes, began to

set the table for the second course, and their hostess took the opportunity to interrupt.

"Well, that was quite lively," said Mrs Haddington. "But perhaps we shall speak of something else during our second course. I can't talk of only banks at Christmas. It does not seem at all fitting for the season!"

Miss Guppy made a sound of dissent, which Louisa-Margaretta thought rather disagreeable. People might mistake Mama for the silliest sort of hostess when in fact she was only trying to be hospitable. There was no chance at all that she did not have an opinion on the subject.

"Miss Guppy," said Louisa-Margaretta through gritted teeth. "I am quite sorry that you did not have a chance to express your own opinion. Do you have a solution in mind?"

Miss Guppy looked over the dishes, which were being whisked away. "Well, I'm not sure I—"

Louisa-Margaretta smiled. "Do tell us, how would you solve this matter of failing banks?"

Louisa-Margaretta had half a mind to go to bed. It had been a dull evening, and she was weary thinking that she would have to spend every such evening in that manner until the seventh of January. Mr Blackmore's conversation had been the only bright spot, but that suspicious old lady had seemed intent on separating them.

Just as Louisa-Margaretta frowned, thinking about her dislike for Mrs Crampton, she saw the very woman look about her furtively before slipping into a ballroom at the end of the hall. Louisa-Margaretta, sure that Mrs Crampton was stealing, rushed to the end door of the ballroom. If she peeked through it carefully, she was sure the inhabitant would not notice, as the passageway was dark.

As she looked in, Louisa-Margaretta noted two people in the room. There was Mrs Crampton, of course, but she was having a rather brazen conversation with Mr Lush.

"I have greater resources than you might think, young man," she heard Mrs Crampton say. "In fact, I expect that I am soon to come into a little money, though my position in the world will still be a precarious one. And as I know little of such things, I would be much obliged if you would help me dispose of it."

There was a pause. "I am quite sorry, madam. I had no idea you wished for my aid," said Mr Lush. "Of course I may assist you! And in your lifetime, with my assistance, you shall become a very rich woman."

"Ah, you flatter me, Mr Lush." Her voice was gentle.

"Indeed, I do not! You have chosen wisely."

"Have I? I've half a mind to bury half my coin in the garden then give you the other half. That is, when I receive it."

His laughter was as smooth as silk. "There is no need, madam. What an opportunity would thereby be wasted! Bury it in the garden, indeed. You had much better trust me with all of it. I can make it grow without getting it dirty. Now, how sure are you of this windfall?"

Mrs Crampton gave a hollow laugh. "Well might you ask. There are still a few cards to be played, but I am reasonably certain."

Louisa-Margaretta smiled grimly. Judith, with her insistence on seeing everyone as a child of God, had missed the truth about Mrs Crampton. She was, quite plainly, counting on receiving a great deal more money from the Guppy family and perhaps from the Blackmores as well. Louisa-

Margaretta, who had never had to fend for herself in that regard, would have admired Mrs Crampton's resourcefulness had she not found her methods most despicable.

"Well, then," said Mr Lush. "I shall arrange for you to leave it all with me at your earliest convenience. At your age, you ought not to be troubled with such things."

"I quite agree," said Mrs Crampton. "And, young man, perhaps you will allow me to wander off to my bed. It has been a trying day, and my bones will not tolerate another moment of toil."

Mr Lush laughed but only for a moment. His mirth was smothered as soon as it began. "Very good, madam. Of course."

Louisa-Margaretta waited, breathless, until she was sure that both of them were gone. Mr Lush, no doubt, had returned to the company of the gentlemen. It was the first time she had heard him speak for so long with a woman.

All she had heard from the Guppy and Blackmore ladies was that Mrs Crampton was a genteel lady who had fallen on hard times and that she used her skill in the healing arts as a means of supporting herself and her children. But as with so many charlatans, it appeared that the healing was merely a ruse. It was a means of gaining entrance into prominent families then asking for ever more generous gifts.

And Judith had probably been right in her other warning too. Mrs Crampton likely meant to target the Haddingtons next. In fact, perhaps she already had.

If they were still in company, Louisa-Margaretta reflected, neither of her parents would listen to her warnings. But she hoped that she might find that at least one of them, probably her father, was ready to retire. If she spoke to them alone, without any Guppy or Blackmore interlopers, they might be more inclined to listen.

Indeed, when she reached her parents' rooms, Papa answered her knock. Her mother, presumably, was still entertaining. He was dressed for bed but with a candle still lit, and he invited his daughter in.

"What is it, Lou?" he asked, plainly baffled by her visit.

"Papa," she said. "Judith gave me a warning earlier, and I thought I ought to let you know."

Something she could not quite read passed over his features. "Very well. I am listening."

Louisa-Margaretta looked around carefully then lowered her voice. "That Mrs Crampton," she said. "She is getting all she can from Mrs Guppy, but Judith supposed she might be after our money too. And from what I just heard, I am now certain."

Her father frowned. "What exactly did you hear, then?"

"She is expecting to come into money," hissed Louisa-Margaretta. "She had some foolish story about an inheritance, and I did not believe it for one moment."

Her father only smiled, looking pleased but puzzled. "Well, she isn't expecting any great sum from our family, I am sure. Though if she won't be offended, when the widows of the village come Thomasing, I shall set aside a sum for her. Your mother will know how best to go about it."

Louisa-Margaretta gave an exasperated sigh. Putting aside a little sum for Mrs Crampton, at just the time when the impoverished ladies of the community customarily came to the door, would certainly not suffice. And Mama had little to do with it. Louisa-Margaretta was not asking her father to rely on his wife, as he always did, but to guard against a very real danger.

"Keep in mind, Papa," she said, "I am sure our family matters not one jot to Mrs Crampton. She would give that pitiful smile then wheedle our last farthing from us."

Her father shook his head. "We are hardly on our last farthing, Lou."

Louisa-Margaretta's face burned. She recalled the conversation she had overheard earlier in the day between Papa and Mr Lush. Her father would tell the stranger all his business troubles, but with her, he went on pretending that he was as rich as he had ever been!

"I oughtn't to think of such things, I suppose, because I am a woman," said Louisa-Margaretta. "You do not trust my capacity for understanding, but you took Sherborne on as your right hand in the business when he was much younger than I am now!"

"Lou," said her father, shaking his head, "listen. I only took Sherborne. Not any of my other sons."

"Why?" asked Louisa-Margaretta.

"They had no interest," said her father. "And you haven't either, at least not until now. Do you wish to accompany me to one of my factories in Manchester? I have been postponing a visit due to our guests, but I ought to go in the new year. And you know Sherborne. As soon as he gets back to London, he won't want to come here again."

Louisa-Margaretta sighed. "No, Papa, I suppose not."

He gave her an indulgent smile. "Then do not worry about Mrs Crampton or about any other financial interests. The reason we have this monstrous home is because I have a good enough head on my shoulders, even if I'm not quite as clever as you are."

Louisa-Margaretta frowned. "You are not fond of Wycliff Castle?"

"I don't complain," said her father. "But it's too many rooms for a little family. Even with guests, the scale of this place is silly."

She was silent for a moment. She had never heard her

father speak glowingly of their home, that was true enough. But she had always assumed that he was the driving force behind its purchase. After all, he had grown up in poverty, and one might assume that he would wish to show the world that he had made his fortune.

It seemed, however, that was not the correct assumption.

Or perhaps he was simply trying to prepare her for a day when their fortunes would turn and they might be forced to sell. If she listened to Sherborne, rather than her father, it appeared that day might be on its way very soon.

"Good night, Papa," she said, favouring him with one of her brightest smiles.

But her heart remained troubled.

17

"I wish we could have waited until dear Percival and Peggy had joined us," said Mrs Haddington. "But then some of you would have left. So we thought it best to have a gathering now."

"We are much indebted to you, I am sure," said Mrs Guppy, though her face looked pinched and anxious. She kept going back to the corner where her elder daughter, Mrs Blackmore, sat carefully with her feet up. Since only a few of the guests had arrived, Louisa-Margaretta was privy to the conversation between Mrs Guppy and Mrs Crampton.

"Nancy has been feeling ill," said Mrs Guppy. "She ought to go back to her room."

"Your daughter needs to feel herself a part of Christmas," said Mrs Crampton firmly. "Her room will be there whenever she might need it."

Louisa-Margaretta watched her mother leave off welcoming the guests and go speak to Mrs Blackmore. The young woman's face brightened, and Louisa-Margaretta saw her mama affectionately touching Mrs Blackmore's arm before she left her. For a moment, Louisa-Margaretta felt less angry at her mother for inviting such ill-tempered guests to their home. Mama loved helping others at Christmas, and if Mrs Blackmore had stayed in her home, she probably would not have enjoyed the holiday at all.

Mr Lush was nearby, holding court with his preferred admirers. Judith had joined the group of gentlemen and was nodding politely as Mr Lush spoke about his travels. Her travels to Russia were doubtless more eventful, but Louisa-Margaretta was sure Mr Lush would not ask about them at all. As a rule, people thought Judith dull when she was merely soft-spoken. They often made the same mistake with Louisa-Margaretta's father.

Indeed, Papa was silent, though he was stroking his chin with a half smile on his face as Mr Lush went on about the beauty of the coastline.

"When you arrive in South America, it looks untamed yet perfect," Mr Lush said. "Much like this painting here! If I am not mistaken, this could be very near where I landed. And I cannot tell you how much I admire how this painter has captured the light just here. He is very accomplished, indeed! And to render the trees with such detail yet while conveying the overall spirit of the place... As soon as I saw this painting the other day, I knew it was done by an expert hand."

"I believe this is a depiction of the south of France," said Judith quietly.

Mr Lush raised his eyebrows. "Have you yourself been to South America, Miss St Clair? Or France, for that matter?"

Judith reddened. "No," she said quickly. "Though someday, I very much hope, perhaps I may be so fortunate—"

"No need to take unnecessary risks," said Mr Lush gallantly.

Louisa-Margaretta saw her father hiding a smile. He

knew that Judith was well traveled, of course, and that even her life in England had been far from uneventful. But he was not going to say so in front of an unappreciative audience such as Mr Lush.

Apparently, Papa was not the only gentleman who was finding all the talk of South America rather tedious. Louisa-Margaretta was not at all displeased when Mr Blackmore left the group of gentlemen and sought her out.

"Miss Haddington," he said, "you look divine. Are you excited for this little party?"

Louisa-Margaretta could not hold back a smile. The man could have said she looked "well" or perhaps "excellent," but he had chosen the word "divine" instead. She could hardly think of a better compliment.

"Of course," she said. "I always enjoy the company of handsome gentlemen at this time of year."

He did not know what to make of her statement, and Louisa-Margaretta enjoyed his distress almost as much as she had enjoyed his cheer. But alas, his sister came striding over and quickly engaged the two of them in a conversation about London gatherings.

"This is ever so much better," she said. "Some of the London parties are both large and crowded. Wycliff Castle is one of the loveliest places I have ever stayed. One could never run out of room here!"

Mr Blackmore, summoned by Mr Lush, walked over to the part of the room where the gentlemen were conversing. He gave Louisa-Margaretta and his sister a brief nod as he walked off. Louisa-Margaretta took care not to sigh. She liked Miss Blackmore, but it was most vexing that her little tête-à-tête had been interrupted in favour of a conversation about parties.

"I would love to go to a London party," said Louisa-Margaretta, "even though I always used to hate them. To see someone besides my immediate neighbors!"

18

"Your immediate neighbors are not *so* terrible, surely," said Judith, joining Louisa-Margaretta and her companion. "Good evening, Miss Blackmore."

Miss Blackmore gave an understanding smile. "Good evening, Miss St Clair. Miss Haddington was just asking me about London parties. There were some literary salons that were very interesting. I used to meet all sorts of people there."

Louisa-Margaretta nodded. "Judith would enjoy those, though I imagine there is a little too much liquor for her taste. I myself have never been a great reader."

Miss Blackmore's face shone. "I must confess, I understand very little of literature, but I enjoy the company. My brother only allows me to go to such gatherings in his presence, though, and since he is hardly literary, I attend them less often than I would like."

Judith looked across the room at Mr Blackmore, who was having a terse conversation with his wife. She was standing, shifting from one foot to another, but he did not appear to notice her discomfort. He was certainly not suggesting that she sit down again. It surprised Judith to hear that he was so protective of his sister.

"Your brother is very attentive, then," she said, making sure that no doubt was present in her voice.

"Oh, not at all," said Miss Blackmore. "It is our mother who insists, and every so often, he's in good enough humour to be bribed."

Louisa-Margaretta watched Mr Blackmore without attending much to the conversation, though Judith wished she would pay attention. After hearing Mr Blackmore's flaws enumerated, perhaps Louisa-Margaretta would no longer pay quite so much attention to the gentleman who had plainly caught her eye.

"I'm glad he was in good humour before your visit," said Judith firmly. "We can discuss literature here, as well, though I am sorry to say that Mr Ramsbury and I may be the only people who are truly fond of books."

"That wouldn't trouble me at all," said Miss Blackmore. "Oh, I nearly forgot! There was one gentleman at the latest gathering who asked to be remembered to you."

Judith gave the room a quick glance, making sure that nobody would be listening to their conversation, as the exuberant Miss Blackmore apparently never spoke quietly. Over the years, Judith had formed acquaintances with many gentlemen whom the Haddingtons might find objectionable, and she hoped that Miss Blackmore would not speak of any of her actor acquaintances. Or, still worse, the scandal-ridden Duke of Ormonde.

"How kind of you to pass on the message," she said politely.

"Oh, I beg your pardon, Miss St Clair. The message was not for you. It was for Miss Haddington, from a Mr Rodrigo. A Mr Isaac Rodrigo, I believe? I didn't get much of a chance to speak with him, but I believe that was his name."

19

Louisa-Margaretta's attention, which had wandered, was yanked back into the room with Miss Blackmore's shocking statement.

"Mr Rodrigo," she repeated, her mind working frantically to find a proper response.

"Yes, he said he knew you from—I forget what it was, some museum. He was very interested to learn that I would be staying with you and begged to be remembered to you. He inquired very pointedly after your family, but since I wasn't yet acquainted with any of you, I had to ask my brother whether your parents and brothers were all well. And I'm afraid he didn't know either!"

"Thank you for passing those messages along," said Judith, and Louisa-Margaretta could see the worry etched across her friend's face.

"Yes, thank you," said Louisa-Margaretta briskly. "Fancy your meeting Mr Rodrigo! I haven't seen him in years."

"As I was saying, one meets so many people in London," said Miss Blackmore. "But it gets to be a bit tedious after a while. There are so very many names, I have to write down a great deal of them as soon as I learn them, and even then, I am rather hopeless."

"You only need stay near Mrs Haddington," said Judith kindly. "She never forgets the name of anyone to whom she has been introduced. Is not that so, Louisa-Margaretta?"

"What?" said Louisa-Margaretta. "Well, yes, I'm sure. You must excuse me."

She walked out of the room, into the passageway, pausing only when she saw that a gentleman was standing beneath the prayer ball. It was not a wise time for her to stand in silence or run off and cry. She had never really been one for weeping, anyway. So instead, she slipped back into the role of the hostess's attentive daughter and began to make polite conversation with Mr Blackmore.

"I thought I could convince Mama to replace it with a kissing ball," said Louisa-Margaretta meaningfully, the knot in her chest easing as she forced herself to smile. "That would be much more lovely during this season, you know."

She saw Mr Blackmore's eyes flicker down the passageway to the room where the company was assembled, but he made no move to join them.

"I'm sure more than one gentleman would be pleased by that addition," he said, gazing into her eyes.

Louisa-Margaretta wasn't fooled. She had experienced true love once then lust and infatuation several times after. She knew that she wasn't in love with Mr Blackmore, not in the sense of true devotion. His was not a name she would embroider into a cushion or say with reverence or even think on with regret after the new year came and the visit was over.

But it would be something to kiss a handsome gentleman again. Especially one who was moving slightly closer but clearly needed a bit more persuasion.

"The nights are so very dark at this time of year," continued Louisa-Margaretta. "One needs a bit of warmth."

What one needs is a distraction, she thought. *Something to take away some of the fear, the twin possibilities of loneliness and poverty.*

But even as a mere distraction, Mr Blackmore would do nicely. Louisa-Margaretta took a step closer.

Before she could see whether he was amenable to her advances, however, two maids ran through the hallway. Louisa-Margaretta took a step back, staring after them.

"I cannot think of a time that I have seen a maid run through this house," she said. "Perhaps the Christmas spirit is rather too strong."

Mr Blackmore, however, was immediately nervous.

"It might be Nancy, my wife," he said hastily. "For them to be running, it must be some sort of disaster."

Louisa-Margaretta straightened up. There was nobody she wished to hear about less than the absent Mrs Blackmore.

"Birth is not a disaster," she said shortly. "Everyone who ever lived was born. Besides, Mama and Judith have attended plenty of women."

She did not succeed in concealing her disgust about the whole process. Even when Louisa-Margaretta admitted to herself that she might like to have one or two children, provided the right father could be found, which was unlikely, the thought of all that blood made her want to pass off a foundling as her own. After all, she wished to hunt and ride, not subject her body to the indignities of childbirth.

In an instant, both Louisa-Margaretta's parents came out, and Mr Blackmore retreated into the shadows. Louisa-Margaretta, however, chose to follow them.

"It must have just happened," her mother was saying. "He looked well enough earlier."

"Good that he cried out," her father said. "If he did. Otherwise, we might not have known."

Mrs Haddington did not break her stride, but she did look pointedly at her husband. "We ought not to accuse the man of any such improprieties until he's cold in his grave."

Louisa-Margaretta was not sure what her parents meant, but she followed them, hoping to find out. It sounded very much as if a man were dead and possibly in rather scandalous circumstances.

Mr Haddington plainly did not agree, although with his wife, he was always deferential.

"Went to his room," he said. "And a young girl found him."

His wife sighed. "I don't completely disagree, my dear. But we can't possibly mention it to anyone until we are sure."

"I'm sorry," said Louisa-Margaretta, struggling to keep up with her parents. They were not running, but they were walking as quickly as they possibly could. "Is anyone going to tell me what has happened?"

For just a moment, Mrs Haddington paused.

"Mr Lush has died," she said. "We are going to his room to see him, but the maids were quite sure."

Louisa-Margaretta frowned, and her parents kept walking. They were quickly nearing the bedroom where Mr Lush had been staying.

"Stay here, Lou," said Mr Haddington, frowning.

Louisa-Margaretta was thankful for her father's order, as she had no wish to go into Mr Lush's room and see his body. Though it did feel a bit eerie, standing outside the door, waiting for her parents to confirm the rumour. They were in the room for only a moment before they came back out. They conferred very briefly with the footmen who had been staying with Mr Lush. Or rather, what had once been Mr Lush. Mrs Haddington was solemn, but she did not reach for a handkerchief. As a rule, in spite of her strong emotions, she was not prone to tears when her powers as a hostess were required.

Mr Haddington had a question for his wife when they emerged.

"That needle sticking out of his body," he said. "Is it the sort of thing one would use for embroidery?"

Louisa-Margaretta blanched at the description, but Mrs Haddington said only "No, for knitting."

"Hmm," said Papa.

Louisa-Margaretta wondered what he was thinking, but as usual, he did not say.

"I'll tell everyone," Mrs Haddington said. "We can move our houseguests to the music room. I'm afraid everyone else will have to leave."

"I'll meet them there," said Mr Haddington.

Louisa-Margaretta noted that he did not seem shocked, only sad.

"Very well," said Mrs Haddington, taking the moment to touch her husband's hand.

It was hardly the time for great shows of affection. Then again, Louisa-Margaretta had noticed that her parents were always united in the face of any crisis. It served them well, although she found it most off-putting when the crisis was, for example, her engagement to a man they considered unsuitable. After Louisa-Margaretta had told her parents that she was going to marry Mr Isaac Rodrigo, she never once heard them quarrel. Instead, their London house was closed, their things packed, and the whole family was off to

Derbyshire before Louisa-Margaretta could get any answers from her parents. Mr Haddington traveled ahead of the ladies, forcing Louisa-Margaretta's brother Loftus to stay with them. By the time they reached Wycliff Castle, it had been purchased and prepared.

The whole thing would have been rather impressive, but Louisa-Margaretta found even the memory maddening. It was a most troubling reminder of her impotence.

"What am I to do?" she complained.

Her mother started. "Oh, my dear. Well, you ought to go to the music room with your father. See to it that Miss St Clair plays, and do your best to keep everyone entertained. I shan't be long."

20

The atmosphere in the music room should have been more cheerful and warm. After all, the fire was roaring, the decor was beautiful, and Judith's strictly metered renditions of Christmas carols on the pianoforte were in keeping with the season. But everyone was frowning, speaking in tones that were perfectly funereal. Mr Lush's death, it seemed, had followed them.

"I know it was a shock," said Judith gently.

"Yes," said Louisa-Margaretta. "It certainly isn't every day that someone dies from poison in this house, although I will admit, it appears to be more common here than anywhere else in England."

Judith winced, thinking of Louisa-Margaretta's aunt. Poor Aunt Matilda had been poisoned at a larger gathering some years ago, and she came into Judith's thoughts every Christmas.

"That isn't what I was speaking of," said Judith. "It was the mention of Mr Rodrigo—"

"I didn't know he was in London, that's all," said Louisa-Margaretta. "I thought he was still in New York."

Judith remembered how alarmed Louisa-Margaretta had once been by any mention of Morgan's name. Her discomfort, over the course of their time apart, had only grown.

"It's very natural that you should feel disturbed by it," she said quietly.

"Nonsense," said Louisa-Margaretta. "It is all in the past. He has a wife now, though I didn't hear Miss Blackmore mention anything about her. Perhaps she's not the literary type."

"Or perhaps she is simply indifferent to gatherings where the primary purpose is to discuss art and literature," said Judith. *As are you*, she added silently.

Louisa-Margaretta sniffed. "I have managed rather nicely since he jilted me. I have learnt a new profession, perfected my French, and gone to the continent. Oh, and broken an engagement. I am sure all London is speaking of that."

"I rather doubt it," said Judith, her solicitude turning fast to annoyance. "There are a great deal of soldiers without work, not to mention people who cannot afford to live well under these current economic conditions."

Louisa-Margaretta, as usual, missed the reference to the plight of the masses and thought only of herself.

"Sherborne is still very worried," she confessed. "Papa tells me that all will yet be well, but I'm not sure I believe him."

Judith looked over at Mr Haddington. He was listening to his wife speak, outwardly appearing undisturbed by the night's events.

"Your father would know," she said. "Your brother, while he may have some ability, does not have your father's experience in these matters."

"We may have to sell Wycliff Castle," said Louisa-Margaretta. "Ha! I guess that will be enough gossip to replace whatever people are saying about Mr Solier and me."

At that, Judith stopped playing. She noticed a stir in the room, so she started up again with some Bach that she could go through easily, even without using any part of her mind or memory. It calmed her. A very little bit.

"Sell your home," she breathed. "Are you quite sure?"

Louisa-Margaretta nodded gravely. "Papa has been hinting about it. I suppose he feels he ought to prepare me, though I know that Mama is the one who loves it most."

Judith privately agreed. Though the Haddingtons had purchased Wycliff Castle almost on a whim, intending to keep Louisa-Margaretta far away from an "unsuitable" engagement with Isaac Rodrigo while maintaining a residence close to Mr Haddington's businesses in Manchester, it was plain how much Mrs Haddington had come to love the place. The village was small, so she could always be of use to its inhabitants, and her status as the patron ensured that her attentions would be received with gratitude. Outward gratitude, at least. Mrs Haddington was never adept at seeing when her attentions were *not* wanted, and Judith knew that more than one family had suffered from feeling unable to send her away.

Mr Haddington appeared to enjoy entertaining his children and their families at Wycliff Castle, but he was often to be found in Manchester. And Louisa-Margaretta, though she appreciated Judith's company and loved the freedom of hunting or riding every day, tended to complain if she was in Derbyshire for more than a fortnight. No, it was Mrs Haddington who was most at home there.

Judith's concern was not merely altruistic, of course. If

the Haddingtons could be convinced to move to smaller quarters and merely let Wycliff Castle to the right sort of family, her father would be able to retain his position. But if they were to sell it, the new patrons might decide that the living ought to be held by someone else. Or perhaps worse, they could change the terms in order to keep Judith's father in his position but severely curtail the tithes he would receive. Judith knew that her papa would not abandon his flock, no matter what the pay. But even if he could find a curate to replace Mr Barnwell, he would not be able to afford one if the new owners were stingy.

Before Judith could worry any more about her father, he arrived. With a nod to her, he went straight over to the Haddingtons, and it took only a moment of conferring before Mrs Haddington addressed the crowd.

"My dear guests," she said. "I know you are probably all eager to get to bed. Mr St Clair has kindly agreed to lead us in prayer, and after that, we should all get some rest."

She then proceeded to speak for several minutes about the tragedy that had befallen the poor young Mr Pembroke Lush, the blessings the Lord had brought them in the holy season, and the impossibility of knowing God's will. By the time Mr St Clair reached the actual prayer, which was brief, it was rather like a postscript to Mrs Haddington's long-winded assertions.

Before she went over to join her father, Judith touched Louisa-Margaretta's arm. "I'll see you in the morning," she said.

Morgan was waiting near them to wish Judith good night, and Louisa-Margaretta only glared.

"Perhaps," she said.

21

After Mr St Clair and Judith's departure, the evening might well have ended. But Mr Guppy seemed glad to be unencumbered by the presence of a clergyman.

"Very well," he said. "Someone must tell me how we are going to get our money."

Mrs Guppy flinched. "My dear, really. Now is not the time."

"Now is exactly the time," said her husband. "Mr Lush took plenty from all of us, and he promised to make us rich. Now, perhaps he may not have had time to invest it all. I've no idea. But I'm damned if I'm going to sit by and watch everything disappear, to be gambled away by some distant cousin of his. I beg your pardon, ladies," he said at the sight of Mrs Haddington's disapproving stare.

Louisa-Margaretta's mother did not smile, but she gave him a curt nod. "I'm sure my husband has it well in hand. It does seem like an odd time to speak of business, but I suppose that we may as well. If the ladies would like to accompany me…"

"An excellent idea," said Mrs Crampton. "This discourse could easily become distressing for all of us."

"I'll stay, thank you," said Louisa-Margaretta. She wished that there were better refreshments in the room.

Her father was shrinking back, Mr Guppy looked red enough that he could lose his temper at any moment, and Mr Blackmore had plainly just thought about the strange complication. And while Cousin Morgan hated even the appearance of avarice, Louisa-Margaretta noticed that his hands were clasped together tightly. All of the warmth and relaxation that his chaste farewell to his fiancée had brought him was well and truly gone.

"Louisa-Margaretta, please come join us," said her mama, but in front of company, it would have been rude to argue more. Louisa-Margaretta, knowing that she could get away with a bit of disobedience, simply settled into her seat and smiled.

Mr Blackmore ran his hands through his lovely hair, his face looking worthy of a romantic painting even in its current panicked state.

"There is no way to know exactly where Mr Lush put the money," he said, "or what each of us is entitled to."

"We can sort it," said Mr Haddington shortly. "We'll speak with my attorneys in Manchester."

"Oh dear," said Cousin Morgan. "I'm not sure that attorneys need to be involved."

It was a rather ironical comment, though Cousin Morgan had not meant it that way. He had once decided to study law himself, though in pursuit of a career as a barrister, not an attorney. Like so many other young men, he gave up those studies once he understood the many pitfalls of a barrister's work. It was just as well, as Louisa-Margaretta could hardly think of anyone less suited to such a profession. Cousin Morgan was honest, kind, and hopelessly generous. He hated the way that professional barristers delighted more in the cadence of their speeches than the justice of their cause. He also had no patience for the many attorneys and solicitors who were more concerned with payment than morality.

"My attorneys already know of Mr Lush," said Mr Haddington. "They are the only people who can definitively advise us."

He did not add anything else. Mr Haddington, though he rarely spoke, was used to being obeyed, and Louisa-Margaretta noticed that even Mr Guppy fell in line.

"Very well," he said. "These attorneys, then, we must see them in the morning."

"Tomorrow?" said Cousin Morgan. "It's almost Christmas."

"All the more reason," insisted Mr Blackmore, agreeing immediately with his father-in-law. "We should see them and get all of this settled."

Mr Haddington only nodded. "Very well, then."

He left quietly, probably to report back to his wife and see about the travel arrangements.

Louisa-Margaretta felt rather sick. The assembled company, apart from Morgan, did not know her father well. They saw only a quiet man, and they would not be able to read joy or sorrow from his still and stoic face.

But Louisa-Margaretta knew better. Papa, it seemed, was most gravely worried. And that meant she needed to be concerned for her own fate as well.

"Cousin Morgan," she hissed as the other gentlemen made to leave the room.

"Louisa-Margaretta," he said. "Will you be going to Manchester with us?"

"No, I hate Manchester," she said simply. "But I need you to be on your guard."

He blinked. "It is only a visit to your father's attorneys. I'm sure it is not dangerous."

"It is extremely dangerous if there's a killer in the carriage," she said, lowering her voice. "Papa is worried, and he is no fool. You must look after him."

Cousin Morgan smiled. "I'm hardly brilliant at seeing to the safety of others," he said, perhaps alluding to his long period fleeing from French law after his travels from Vienna had gone wrong. "But of course I will do my best."

"And if he gets ill, don't let that Mrs Crampton see him," she hissed.

Cousin Morgan drew himself up as if surprised. "If he gets ill? What, your father?"

Mr Haddington's health was generally excellent, but Louisa-Margaretta nodded vigorously.

"Yes. She probably came here because she was after his money, and she'll want to take advantage. You can't allow it."

Cousin Morgan looked more amused than concerned, which Louisa-Margaretta found infuriating, but he nodded.

"If your father falls ill, I will tend to him myself," he said. "But I don't think you need to worry about him, Louisa-Margaretta."

"Well, you're a fool," she said plainly. "Until that woman is out of our house, I shall worry about both my parents. For all we know, she is behind Mr Lush's death. Perhaps she wished to poison him then charge him some grand sum of money for the cure, and it all went wrong. Perhaps he refused to pay!"

She left the room, fuming, to the sound of Cousin Morgan's laughter. At least someone was happy, she thought.

She herself would not be happy or content until every last Crampton, Guppy, and Blackmore had left Wycliff Castle. They were a bad omen, bringing only misfortune, and in spite of Mr Blackmore's very handsome face, Louisa-Margaretta could not help but wish them gone.

22

The household was a flurry of activity first thing in the morning. Mrs Haddington had probably risen before them all, and she was striding all over the castle, giving stern orders to servants and guests alike. It had been some years since Louisa-Margaretta had risen early enough to know when exactly her mother awakened, but she was rather sure it was much earlier than she would like.

It was all settled—only the gentlemen were to go. Like most instances when her presence was rejected on the basis of her sex, Louisa-Margaretta felt a sense of injustice. However, she could think of few pursuits more dull than suffering a cold, bumpy carriage ride all the way to Manchester. At journey's end, there would be only a meeting with some attorneys. And it wouldn't be journey's end, not really, as weather permitting, the gentlemen would all come back the same day. It was no wonder most of them hadn't left the comforts of Wycliff Castle yet. They were probably regretting their hasty decision to travel.

Louisa-Margaretta called for her outdoor garments, wondering if one gentleman in particular might desire her company. By lingering in the front parlor, Louisa-Margaretta was able to watch the preparations that took place outdoors without joining in. First the carriage was brought around then warmed, as the horses stamped in the cold, their steaming breath vanishing in the misty Derbyshire morning.

Louisa-Margaretta was in luck. Her father and Mr Guppy were nowhere to be seen. Only Mr Blackmore went out, though he lingered, staring at the carriage.

Louisa-Margaretta followed not long after.

"Good morning, Mr Blackmore," she said. "I am glad that I woke up in time to wish you a good journey."

He frowned. "Well, it will not be an easy journey, I think. I would rather stay, but my father-in-law wished me to go. He is always very interested in these legal matters."

"Manchester is rather horrid at this time of year," Louisa-Margaretta agreed. "And the journey can be very dull."

"I am sorry that we shall not be able to ride together, Miss Haddington," said Mr Blackmore.

The poor man looked so distressed that Louisa-Margaretta felt pity for him.

Pity, perhaps, and something else.

"Go ahead into the carriage," she said. "You'll catch your death out here."

He looked disappointed to be parted from her then pleased when she followed him in.

"I know it is unexpected," said Louisa-Margaretta. "But you needn't worry. Papa always finds a way to get through any business difficulty."

She knew well that she was trying to convince herself, not him. In her lifetime, prices had risen and fallen, wars had started and ended, and yet Louisa-Margaretta had never seen her father's fortunes truly fall. Either he had some brilliance, which the size of his fortune might well imply, or he'd had a run of very good luck.

"It's not that, precisely," said Mr Blackmore. "I'm quite sure that the money I gave to Mr Lush is safe, and if the investments do not come through immediately, well, I am sure my fortunes will survive."

Louisa-Margaretta brightened. "Well, what is it, then? Are you simply mourning the loss of a friend?"

"We were not great friends," said Mr Blackmore. "I think he liked me well enough, but he seemed to prefer older men, like your father."

Richer men, thought Louisa-Margaretta, but she said nothing.

"What troubles you, then?" she asked, her face the picture of respectful but deep interest in the gentleman's concerns.

She knew that concern and interest, when employed in concert, could often be the way to a gentleman's heart.

"This whole journey is not what I had in mind at all, not for Christmas," said Mr Blackmore. "Begging your pardon, Miss Haddington. Wycliff Castle is very lovely indeed."

Louisa-Margaretta only smiled. "What is troubling you, sir? I assure you, I shall not be offended."

"Well," he said. "I haven't seen any of the men from my club in ages. There is almost no sport to be had here, and nobody cares at all what I do. I suppose I once hoped that, once I were master of my own life, I should have holidays that were more fun. Not dull ones, if you'll pardon me."

"We shall have to see to it that your Christmas is anything but dull," she teased.

Mr Blackmore blinked. "How would you make sure of that, Miss Haddington?"

Louisa-Margaretta heard her mother walking out of Wycliff Castle, shouting more instructions to the coachmen. That alone ought to have startled her into leaving the carriage, but instead, she claimed one last moment alone with Mr Blackmore.

And she kissed him.

It was not a lengthy embrace, as they were pressed for time, but it was long enough for Louisa-Margaretta to feel Mr Blackmore's surprise change to delight. He stared at her as she leapt out of the carriage.

"Mama," Louisa-Margaretta said, trying and failing to keep a grin off her face. "Have you seen to all the hampers? There is nothing decent to eat between here and Manchester, after all."

Mrs Haddington, who typically kept a sharp watch on her daughter, might well have noticed Louisa-Margaretta's flushed cheeks and wide smile. But her eyes were trained instead on Judith, who was coming quickly up the walk to meet them.

"Miss St Clair," said Mrs Haddington, the barest acknowledgement of Judith's presence she could give without publicly snubbing her rector's daughter.

"Mrs Haddington, good morning," said Judith, all politeness. She rushed over to greet Louisa-Margaretta.

"We should go inside," murmured Judith. "It's very cold this morning."

Louisa-Margaretta glanced at the carriage again. She had been hoping for a last glimpse of Mr Blackmore before the gentlemen departed, but she realised it would be wiser to follow her friend.

"Very well," she said. "But we must come back out again soon. You'll feel perfectly well once you're in a riding habit, Judith, especially if we can find you the right horse."

Louisa-Margaretta was almost as pleased to be riding with Judith as she would have felt had Mr Blackmore been unengaged. More pleased, in many ways, for when she was with Judith, Louisa-Margaretta could be completely honest. With Mr Blackmore, she needed to pretend some sort of innocence. She could flirt with him, but she had to say things like, "Oh, that was a clever remark. Do go on" rather than "Dear Mr Blackmore, you are a handsome man who is disenchanted with his wife. Won't you pay me greater attention?" Such a direct approach would certainly have put him off, and Louisa-Margaretta despised any form of subterfuge that forced her to act the part of a vapid young lady.

"What happened between you and Mr Blackmore?" asked Judith, her voice heavy with suspicion.

Louisa-Margaretta was reminded that she could never be completely honest, not even with her old friend.

"Don't trouble yourself, Judith," she said indolently. "He is disappointed to be going to Manchester rather than staying here at Wycliff Castle."

"Here at Wycliff Castle with *you*," said Judith. "Oh, my friend, do take care."

Louisa-Margaretta spurred her horse on, not at all troubled that Judith was struggling to keep up.

"I am plenty careful," she snapped. "This family party is rather dull, and you are seldom with us. Mr Blackmore's company is amusing."

Judith looked as if she were going to say something in response, but she held her tongue.

"Miss Blackmore's company is plenty amusing," Judith said after a moment. "And even Miss Guppy can be pleasing, when she wishes to entertain."

Louisa-Margaretta shook her head. "Another young lady prone to fits of melancholia. It is an epidemic among the better families."

Judith did not have to say the words, as Louisa-Margaretta supplied them herself.

"Including mine," she said. "You can say it, Judith!"

"I did not wish to," said Judith quickly. "Only you have seen many young women suffer in this manner, Louisa-Margaretta, and young men."

"Well, Mrs Crampton ought to cure it," said Louisa-Margaretta. "Though all her remedies couldn't help poor Mr Lush, could they?"

Judith frowned. "You do not believe he was taken ill either, I take it."

Louisa-Margaretta felt pride bloom in her heart. Though she and Judith might disagree on many things, when it came to the little matter of murder, their thoughts were still in concert.

"It is all very suspicious," said Louisa-Margaretta. "He seemed perfectly well a day ago. Even at the beginning of the gathering, I was not apprehensive."

"No," said Judith. "He was truly his usual self, going on about the investment scheme and his plans in London."

"He also had a knitting needle sticking out of his body," said Louisa-Margaretta triumphantly. "I suppose he could have fallen on it by accident, but it seems much more likely he was stabbed."

She was silent for a moment, giving Judith a chance to take in the gruesome news. But even after she frowned, Judith still did not speak.

"What is it?" asked Louisa-Margaretta. "Is there something else you noticed?"

"Well," said Judith. "It seems rather odd that he is here.

Would this not have been an ideal time for him to find investors in London? Many families are on their estates, but those who are not are visiting constantly. He could have gone to dozens of parties like the one your parents hosted yesterday."

Louisa-Margaretta was silent. She remembered her father's assurances. He had never given her a reason to distrust him. Though her father did not speak a great deal, he did not treat her like a child, and besides, it made no sense for him to kill Mr Lush before he saw any return on his five hundred pounds.

"Mr Lush wanted my father's money," she said finally. "I think it is possible that his real target in coming here was my father, not Mr Blackmore or Mr Guppy."

Judith appeared to think on it.

"It is reasonable," she said gently. "Your father has a great deal more to spare. I'm sure Mr Lush stood to earn a great deal of money if your father believed strongly in his scheme."

Louisa-Margaretta, hearing her friend's heavy breathing, slowed her horse down. They would soon reach a rocky part of the path, and if she urged Godiva on with too much force, the stubborn beast would stop entirely.

"That is the trouble," said Louisa-Margaretta. "I do not know how much Papa has to spare."

Judith looked briefly down the hill then at her horse again. It was plain that she was trying not to smile.

"What?" said Louisa-Margaretta.

"Your parents own Wycliff Castle," said Judith gently. "Even if he did encounter some financial difficulties, would not this home give them some of the resources they might wish for?"

"You seem very untroubled by the prospect of my family's ruin," snapped Louisa-Margaretta, and Judith denied that emphatically.

"Of course I am not," she insisted. "But Mr Lush plainly did not think you were ruined, and I hope that he was right on that point."

"Fine," said Louisa-Margaretta. "Since we are agreed, that leaves the question unanswered. Who would have had a reason to kill Mr Lush?"

"He was found in his bedchamber," said Judith primly.

Louisa-Margaretta waited, but that was apparently all that her friend had to offer.

"And you interpret this to mean what, Judith?"

"If he attempted to force himself on a young lady, she would be within her rights if she needed to defend herself," said Judith quickly.

"But he was stabbed with a knitting needle," said Louisa-Margaretta. "I suppose a young woman could have done that, though I can't think why. It would be very odd for her to bring such a thing into Mr Lush's bedchamber."

"Well," said Judith, "I suppose we could find out."

Louisa-Margaretta laughed, her heart lifting. "And how on earth are we supposed to do that?"

"You can become friends with Miss Guppy. I will endeavor to speak with Miss Blackmore."

Louisa-Margaretta sighed. "Why would you give me Miss Guppy?" she complained. "She hardly ever wishes to speak. It is so dull trying to have a conversation with her."

"Yes, but you have a more exuberant spirit," insisted Judith. "You are more likely to get something from her. Miss Blackmore, it seems, would speak to anyone."

"Yes," said Louisa-Margaretta. "The Blackmore family appears to be rather more forthcoming."

Judith shot her friend a suspicious look, and Louisa-

Margaretta knew they were both thinking of Mr Blackmore. She remembered the brief kiss they had shared in the carriage. There might be very few opportunities for her to see him in such ideal surroundings, but Wycliff Castle was large, as were the woods that surrounded it. After he returned from Manchester, she was sure to think of something.

If only she could first get a few words out of Miss Guppy.

23

Louisa-Margaretta got more than a few words out of Miss Guppy as soon as she got on the topic of Mr Lush. It was rather brilliant, in fact. She cornered Miss Guppy as soon as she returned from her ride. Miss Guppy, who had been sitting near the fire in the morning room with Miss Blackmore, allowed Louisa-Margaretta's presence only reluctantly, while Miss Blackmore flounced off, ostensibly to check on her sister-in-law.

"Poor Mrs Blackmore does not leave her bed," said Louisa-Margaretta. "I should die of boredom."

"I would take to my bed and never leave it if I had to endure another man like Mr Lush," said Miss Guppy. "Papa wanted him to make *me* an offer, but fortunately, he preferred my sister. Me as Mrs Pembroke Lush. Can you imagine?"

In fact, Louisa-Margaretta could imagine that circumstance rather easily. Her own parents, though they wanted her to marry well, sometimes grew impatient with Louisa-Margaretta's spinsterhood. Her mother had been all too ready to see her daughter united to the taciturn and snobbish Mr Solier, though Louisa-Margaretta thought that perhaps Papa might eventually have raised some objection had she not broken off the engagement herself.

"Well, you shan't have to marry him now," said Louisa-Margaretta, but Miss Guppy was not listening.

"He gave up eventually," she said darkly. "After I did take to my bed. I did not leave for a month."

"That was courageous," said Louisa-Margaretta, impressed in spite of herself.

Miss Guppy shook her head. "It was not a conscious choice. But after enduring such horrid suitors, I could not face even the act of walking to the drawing room. Do you know that there was one of them who would speak only with my brother? Every time I asked a question that he thought was difficult or impertinent or unbecoming of a woman, he would turn straight to George. I felt as though I weren't even human."

Judith pondered that. "It's rather odd that he wouldn't answer a simple question from a young lady."

Miss Guppy pouted. "It's like I said, I didn't register as a person, not at all. I was supposed to listen, not question. That's what many men believe."

Louisa-Margaretta had no argument against that, but she would not have responded by taking to her bed.

"You could have said something to him," she said. "I never allow a gentleman to ignore me."

Miss Guppy frowned. "I am not like you and Abigail—Miss Blackmore. I seldom find those words when they are required."

"Well, you got out of bed eventually," said Louisa-Margaretta. "I suppose that's what matters. What inspired you?"

She thought that if Miss Guppy had been cured, she

might be able to use the cure. If the Haddingtons fell into poverty and Louisa-Margaretta needed to go work at the asylum again, a cure for melancholia would be most useful.

Miss Guppy stiffened. "Many things changed. My sister married, and my parents sent me to live with her for a time."

Louisa-Margaretta sighed. "I should have liked to have had a sister. At some point, I am sure my parents will pass me off to one of my brothers, and I am not at all looking forward to it."

"Miss Blackmore is fond of her brother," said Miss Guppy, and Louisa-Margaretta was surprised by the appropriateness of the remark. She was also surprised to find that she hungered for more information about the young man.

"Tell me more about Mr Blackmore," she purred. "Indeed, I feel as if I hardly know him! It would be wonderful to learn more about your family."

24

Judith knew that Mrs Haddington would be far too polite to refuse to feed her at luncheon, particularly if the request came from Morgan. But she had forgotten that he was in Manchester with the others, so Louisa-Margaretta had to beg her mother to add another place for Judith.

Judith did not miss the fact that Louisa-Margaretta had seated herself directly next to Miss Guppy, who for once did not seem to mind the arrangement. Judith endeavored to sit next to Miss Blackmore, so they had ample opportunities for conversation. And Miss Blackmore, as usual, did not disappoint. She had a million stories about London, and she pressed Judith for her own favourite anecdotes, especially stories from her time in Russia and the strange conditions she endured in order to get there.

"I believe my traveling days are nearing an end," said Judith, trying not to allude too directly to her marriage plans for fear Mrs Haddington would hear. "Miss Blackmore, when the weather improves, will you yourself make plans to travel?"

"I am not sure what my plans for the spring are," said Miss Blackmore, her eyes flickering to the end of the table before she looked out the window. "That certainly sounds lovely, though, Miss St Clair."

That interested Judith. For the first time, the open and gregarious young woman appeared to be hiding something. Perhaps it had to do with the spring. And she was reminded of another young woman of her acquaintance, someone who had looked perfectly normal at Christmas but expected to grow large then be delivered of an infant once the weather grew warm.

Naturally, Judith was forced to inquire further.

"Do you wish to travel?" she asked. "I imagine your family is rather scattered."

"Well, no. That is, I enjoy staying with my brother," she said. "And I may stay longer. Because of the, well, the baby, you understand."

She seemed so embarrassed that Judith could not come up with a reasonable explanation. But Miss Blackmore's sudden reaction struck her.

"Are you fond of children, Miss Blackmore?" she asked.

The young lady shrugged. "I suppose everyone is. I mean, isn't it part of every young lady's duty to become a wife and mother? If she is to be fulfilled, that is, in the most natural manner."

Judith tried to hide a smile. She could hardly believe that she was speaking with the same young woman who had boasted of rejecting one proposal after another. Something about the topic of having babies was making Miss Blackmore most uncomfortable, so Judith thought she might as well show mercy and change the discussion.

"I believe that Christmas may be rather subdued," she said. "There is to be a funeral soon, after all. But in the meantime, I would love for you to come visit me at the rectory some morning if you should feel so inclined."

Miss Blackmore immediately brightened. "Oh, could I! That would be lovely."

"Yes," said Judith. She dared not say how unpleasant she was finding the meals she had to take with her father, her brothers, Miriam, and Mr Barnwell. That alone would have been a good enough reason to come to Wycliff Castle as often as she could, even if it were not for the small matter of murder.

"I'm sure my brothers would love to meet you," said Judith, although she hesitated to think about how she would explain Joseph's behavior to a stranger.

"Your sister seemed lovely," said Miss Blackmore. "Miss Miriam St Clair, that was her name? We scarcely had time to speak the other evening."

"Yes," said Judith politely. She noticed that Mrs Haddington was carefully monitoring the discourse at the table. Mrs Blackmore and Mrs Crampton were conversing without paying attention to anyone else. Miss Guppy was glaring down the table, apparently not at all in good humour after her conversation with Louisa-Margaretta.

Judith very much hoped it had been a conversation, not an interrogation.

"Thank you for a delicious meal, Mrs Haddington," said Judith, but as usual, the reception she got was only minimally polite.

"You are all very welcome," said Mrs Haddington, perhaps in order to avoid addressing Judith directly. "Shall we go through to the music room?"

25

The gentlemen were home in time for dinner. Though Louisa-Margaretta was surprised, she was also pleased. After all, she now knew more of Mr Blackmore, and young Mrs Blackmore still kept to her room. It was a wonderful opportunity for the two of them to converse, and when Louisa-Margaretta found herself seated next to him, she was elated. That Cousin Morgan was at her other elbow was unfortunate but not disturbing, she decided. She need not speak with her cousin at all. As a family member, he would be forced to forgive her.

"Tell me," Louisa-Margaretta said as soon as the company was seated and after Mrs Haddington had begun a rather loud discourse on her favourite sermons from Christmases past, "what did you think of Manchester, Mr Blackmore? Or was there any time for sightseeing?"

But the gentleman only scowled. "There was no time for such a thing, no."

Louisa-Margaretta, never one to be easily discouraged by a little rudeness, tried again.

"Papa's attorneys can be rather dull," she said. "But I

hope your conference was not too tedious. Though he does not trust any of them, he does seem to find ways of making them say what they mean."

"I'll thank you not to speak of it, Miss Haddington," said Mr Blackmore.

Louisa-Margaretta noticed that he had not once met her eyes, which she considered the height of rudeness. However, in her experience, most gentlemen were prepared to defend any behavior that did not involve brandishing a weapon or using words unacceptable to a lady's ears.

To test that idea, she asked Mr Blackmore one more question. "Why are you so ill-tempered today, Mr Blackmore?"

If she had hoped to shame him into better manners, her hope was in vain. He still did not meet her eyes, but he took a rather larger gulp of wine than she considered polite.

"What the attorneys had to say was very simple," he said. "There is no such place as Mostiania."

Louisa-Margaretta's expression was just as sour as his. "Is this all the answer I am to expect? That my father's attorneys are ignorant of geography and that vexed you?"

"Louisa-Margaretta," said Cousin Morgan with a delicacy that made her despise him. His gentle tact was almost as unbearable as Mr Blackmore's rudeness. "The country that Mr Lush spoke of does not exist."

"Well, I am sure he did not say it was a country," said Louisa-Margaretta, colouring slightly. "Besides, how could a Manchester man say anything like this for certain?"

"Your father had written to them some days before," said Cousin Morgan. "He wished for more information, and they got it from more than one former sailor. It is not present in any map or the living memory of any man, and Mr Lush's descriptions are utterly unlike anything they would have expected for the general area."

Louisa-Margaretta knew when she was beaten. She took a large bite of her meat as her cousin carefully nibbled at his. Though she had not particularly liked Mr Lush, it pained her to think that she had been taken in with the rest of the fools. The only reason he did not pay attention to her, she realised, was not her sex. If she were a woman in control of her own income, a widow, perhaps, Mr Lush would surely have flattered her just the same way he did with all the men. But because she had nothing of her own, he must have considered such attentions a wasted effort.

"So, what is to become of these investments, then?" she asked.

Her father, near enough to hear, simply shook his head.

Mr Guppy, though, was happy to answer. "You fellows will get your money. Or what we can find of it. He'd had no opportunity to put any of that in the bank, though where he did put it, nobody could say."

"But everyone else?" asked Judith. Just after the words left her mouth, she looked ashamed of her curiosity.

"Nothing," said Mr Haddington. He had a knack for short answers.

"Well, we should see what we can do," said Mrs Haddington. "Within the limits of the law, of course. Did the attorneys provide any guidance as to a possible legal remedy?"

Morgan paled at the question. "They were rather short with us. They said that educated gentlemen ought not to have been taken in by such a scheme. And to be quite honest, I cannot help but agree with them."

Louisa-Margaretta saw Judith take a quick breath,

looking in shame at the tablecloth. Mr Blackmore, on the other hand, was offended at once.

"We did nothing wrong!" he said. "Those fellows, their condescension. I was not going to sit and apologise for being hospitable, nor for seeking to better my position!"

Mrs Crampton frowned in sympathy. "Perhaps, Mrs Haddington, we ought to arrange an outing after the meal. This sort of strain is no good for the constitution."

Mr Blackmore got up from the table. "There is no sense in pretending to eat any more. Not at the same table where we all lost our fortunes."

Louisa-Margaretta noticed that, in spite of Mrs Crampton's sympathetic manner, she did not appear at all surprised. She wondered whether the old woman might have been working in secret with Mr Lush. Judith might know.

But instead of asking her, Louisa-Margaretta was forced to go back to conversing with her cousin. Mrs Haddington, once again, was determined to light upon a topic that did not offend her guests. She chose the scenery of Derbyshire, generally a very agreeable subject, though nobody spoke with much enthusiasm. In fact, Mr Haddington himself had to insert monosyllables when Mrs Haddington spoke with no responses, and she cast her husband many a grateful look for taking on the role in the conversation from all the way down the table.

Louisa-Margaretta kept her voice at a whisper so as not to call attention to her little conference with Cousin Morgan.

"Where could he have put the money?" she asked. "Wouldn't most of it be in a bank?"

Cousin Morgan shook his head bitterly. "Apparently, since there wasn't time, he would have kept it here. But your father and I searched his things last night, and there was almost nothing there."

"Would it all have been in banknotes, then?"

Cousin Morgan shook his head sadly. "I don't keep a great sum with me," he explained. "But I did have a valuable old watch of my father's that I'd intended to sell before the wedding. Mr Lush took it off me, but I can't imagine where he hid it."

"We should search for it, then," said Louisa-Margaretta, fighting the impulse to stand up from her chair.

Cousin Morgan shook his head. "He must have known he would eventually be discovered. Or that there was a risk of it. Wherever my watch is, it's well hidden, and Wycliff Castle is large."

Louisa-Margaretta smirked. "I found that stolen portrait, remember, back when that horrid Duke was visiting," she said, omitting Judith's role in that little incident. "I'm sure I can find a watch."

Cousin Morgan looked uneasily about the table. As a Quaker, he was not supposed to put a great emphasis on material possessions. However, Louisa-Margaretta knew that he was thinking of his future.

"Oh, Louisa-Margaretta, please do look for it," he said in hushed tones, his voice breaking. "If we don't have either that watch or Judith's dowry, we cannot marry."

26

Judith had a servant send word to the rectory that she would be staying at Wycliff Castle. Though Mrs Haddington had not specifically invited her, Louisa-Margaretta had, and there was far too much for them to discuss. Besides, missing one breakfast with Mr Barnwell and Miriam together was probably worth all the hostess's wrath.

First, of course, there was Morgan.

"Cousin Morgan lost a valuable watch to Mr Lush," said Louisa-Margaretta. "Tell me, Judith, with everything he inherited, how he came to have nothing but a lovely little watch to his name."

"His generosity," said Judith, but Louisa-Margaretta hushed her.

"Very well," she said. "But Mr Lush cannot have sold this watch, so it is somewhere in the castle."

"Like most of the money," said Judith. "Oh Louisa-Margaretta, I'm very afraid that all the men are going to fall under suspicion, though I suppose we cannot know who was aware of Mr Lush's fraudulent nature."

"It does not signify who suspects them, as long as it is not that horrid magistrate," said Louisa-Margaretta. "He is going to come tomorrow to speak with everyone. I must tell you, I have never met a ruder gentleman."

"I'm going to tell Mr Fletcher about Mr Lush's occupation," said Judith. "It would be completely unreasonable to keep it from him."

Louisa-Margaretta shook her head. "You will say nothing to Mr Fletcher, the scoundrel."

Judith put a hand on her friend's arm, which Louisa-Margaretta promptly shook off.

"He is not a scoundrel," said Judith. "You must acknowledge at least that much. If he is not a talented magistrate, at least he is an honest man."

Louisa-Margaretta walked over to the window and stared out at the cloudless night sky for a moment before she came back over to Judith.

"My dear friend," she said as if she were speaking to a particularly ignorant child. "Mr Fletcher was ready to arrest all of us for murder last time we encountered him. Mama, though she would never admit it, still snubs the Fletcher family because of the things he said to Cousin Morgan. You wish to speak to this man, admit that your intended was one of his victims, and hope that some sense of honesty or duty will save us all?"

"Everyone lost money," said Judith firmly. "Mr Fletcher cannot very well accuse us all at once."

"No, but he will be sure to settle upon someone in the household," said Louisa-Margaretta. "Rather than reaching some conclusion about suicide, which you must admit would be most convenient for all involved."

"I'm not sure one can commit suicide by falling on a knitting needle," said Judith.

"One can fall on a sword, so I don't see why not. And perhaps, if your entire purpose on God's green earth is to part good people from their coin, you might fall on your needle by an act of divine providence."

"Mr Lush did not deserve to die," said Judith quickly.

"No," said Louisa-Margaretta. "But he did deserve to rot in prison. And given the amount that he stole, he very well may have ended up hanged for theft."

Judith shuddered. "Nobody ought to be hanged for stealing. Hanging itself is a barbaric practice that ought to be abolished entirely."

Louisa-Margaretta rolled her eyes. "Say what you will, I think you were born a Quaker, Judith. At any rate, I am quite sure Mr Fletcher does not agree with such sentiments."

"I must tell him what I know," Judith said firmly.

"Will you tell him about Mrs Crampton?"

Judith drew a breath. "I know nothing definite about Mrs Crampton."

"Don't you?" said Louisa-Margaretta. "You know that Mr Guppy thought she had come along with his family to swindle them and perhaps to get what she could from my family as well."

"Yes," said Judith slowly. "Mr Guppy also does not appear to be subject to any physical complaints. Mrs Crampton is bringing relief and comfort to Mrs Guppy and Mrs Blackmore, surely."

"And perhaps Mr Guppy is able to have a clear-eyed view of Mrs Crampton's scheme."

"I am not sure that we must call helping women with complaints that male healers have neglected a *scheme*, exactly," said Judith.

Louisa-Margaretta shook her head so violently that her braided hair was tossed about. "Judith, consider. There are plenty of gentlemen happy to charge very high fees for working as an accoucheur to a lady who is expecting to be confined soon. It seems that the Guppy family ought to be able to afford such a thing."

Judith hesitated. "They would not have a woman's touch. You remember how things were at the Home with the doctor."

Louisa-Margaretta did remember, Judith was sure, even if she arrived at the Home only after their doctor's untimely death. The asylum, though humane, had employed a male doctor, Mr Fortescue, who had never listened to women. He was dismissive to the point of cruelty with Judith and many of the other ladies, and he particularly ignored any woman to whom he had an obligation. Though Judith had learned after his death that the man had some redeeming qualities, she was not at all surprised that he was not popular among the ladies who either stayed or worked at the asylum.

"I'm not going to say anything against Mrs Crampton," said Judith. "But if you feel your conscience dictates that you tell Mr Fletcher, you must go through with it."

Louisa-Margaretta laughed, and Judith went through the connecting door to the room that had been prepared for her, shivering even in the perfectly warmed bedclothes.

As she tried to sleep, she envied Louisa-Margaretta. For Judith, matters of conscience could easily become a torment, making it feel impossible for her to continue taking the easy path. For Louisa-Margaretta, convenience nearly always trumped morality. If she thought it expedient to speak to Mr Fletcher, she would. If it seemed that such a course would not benefit her, she would not.

Judith could not say what Mr Fletcher would do with the information about the bad investments. And in truth, she could only hope that he would be honest and judicious.

In her previous encounters with him, she had sensed some animosity for the Haddingtons. After all, for all Mrs Haddington's love for Derbyshire, they were relatively new arrivals. They had purchased Wycliff Castle, Louisa-Margaretta in tow, and instantly acquired great power over the entire community.

That power included the ability to take away Judith's father's position. Perhaps she ought to be very careful about how she got away in the morning. As long as Mrs Haddington didn't see her, she ran little risk of offending the grand lady. As soon as she and Morgan left, Judith was certain that she would be safe from future troubles.

If they could leave. Morgan seemed convinced they would not have enough money to marry without his valuable watch or her dowry, and though Judith privately did not agree, she could not force him to take the vows.

It was time for her to convince her father.

27

Louisa-Margaretta was glad that Mr Fletcher called her in with Judith. The latter looked as if she could hardly stand. In spite of Louisa-Margaretta's admonitions, Judith was determined to tell the magistrate about Mr Lush's corruption. But it looked as if she would need some smelling salts before she did so.

"I thought it best to speak to the young ladies together," he said primly. "Miss Guppy would not say two words together until her friend, Miss Blackmore, encouraged her to speak."

"Do not be offended, Mr Fletcher," said Louisa-Margaretta. "Miss Guppy almost never speaks to us either, and we do our best to offer her rather more edifying topics of conversation. I cannot imagine she would have much to say about a murder."

"Why do you suspect murder?" Mr Fletcher was endeavoring, and failing, to keep his voice even, Louisa-Margaretta noted.

Her smile was broad. "My dear sir, I noted the way

everyone in the household panicked when an apparently healthy young man dropped dead for no reason. And if natural causes were to blame, I am certain you would not have expressed a wish to speak with all of us."

"Very well," said Mr Fletcher. "Let's get on with it, then. Did this Mr Lush have any enemies?"

Judith finally stirred to life. "He was taking money from everyone to fund a scheme in a country that did not exist. He called the place Mostiania. Or Mositania. It varied."

Mr Fletcher raised his eyebrows. "Everyone gave him money? Can you provide me with names?"

Judith looked uneasy, and Louisa-Margaretta sighed. Now that her friend had revealed the whole sorry scheme, there was probably no harm in telling him who was involved.

"All of the men here," said Louisa-Margaretta. "They were all fools, apparently. My father, my cousin Mr Ramsbury, Mr Blackmore, and Mr Guppy. Miss St Clair, did your father give him anything?"

"I am sure he did not," said Judith quickly. "He would not have considered it a wise use of resources."

Louisa-Margaretta scoffed. "Quite right."

Mr Fletcher had raised his eyebrows, but he looked skeptical, not impressed.

"Which of them was least able to afford such a thing?" he asked. "I imagine some of them paid the fellow just to make him go away."

Louisa-Margaretta tried not to openly mock Mr Fletcher, but she could not keep herself from saying, "Sir, given the sums of money involved, I think that very unlikely."

"What were the sums, then?"

Judith broke in. "We know no specific numbers. But I am

rather sure that Mr Ramsbury had the least resources of any of them."

Louisa-Margaretta gave a great sigh. Of course Judith would throw her own beloved into the lion's den, all for the sake of honour!

"I am quite sure that you do not wish to repeat your mistakes as concerns my cousin," she said sweetly. "Did Miss St Clair mention that he was trained as a barrister? He is very, *very* familiar with the law."

She knew it to be an exaggeration. Poor Cousin Morgan. He was never meant to be a barrister and would surely have done a horrid job were he ever called upon to perform such duties. But since he had abandoned those studies, there was no way to be sure.

Unfortunately, Mr Fletcher did not appear to be intimidated by dear Cousin Morgan, a man whose timidity ensured that he would eat a bowl of soup with a fork and knife rather than ask for a spoon if one had been forgotten.

"I cannot be fully sure that I was in error," said Mr Fletcher. "An absence of guilt does not necessarily imply innocence."

Louisa-Margaretta felt a quick pressure on her palm. Judith was squeezing her hand, reminding her that Mr Fletcher had never figured out who the real culprit was in the murder he'd once accused Morgan of committing. Judith and Louisa-Margaretta knew, but they could not very well say so without implicating themselves.

Louisa-Margaretta glared at Mr Fletcher. "You have been mistaken in the past. I hope that has taught you plenty of humility. If it has not, I am quite sure that our rector could instruct you in that virtue."

Mr Fletcher was taken aback. "I am sure I do not require

any young women of the neighborhood to comment on my moral instruction."

"Well, you ought to listen to the advice you are given," said Louisa-Margaretta, helping Judith stand and escorting her from the room. "For if you do not, you may very well make *another* grave error."

28

Morgan found Judith as soon as she'd spoken to Mr Fletcher. She held back her tears until they were alone in the library, but as soon as they were out of hearing of the household, she had to pull out her handkerchief. All the memories of the last false accusations against Morgan were foremost in her mind. Though Louisa-Margaretta had brought them up only to mock and chasten Mr Fletcher, they'd had a most unfortunate effect on Judith. She could not bear the thought of any more accusations against her beloved, especially when her only defense was that she knew his character. He would never do something so reprehensible. Unfortunately, her exact words were probably used by every accused man's sweetheart, and they would do nothing to prove either innocence or guilt.

"I am so sorry." She reached for Morgan's hand.

He took her in his arms. It was, perhaps, unwise in their current circumstances, but Judith did not resist. She found comfort in Morgan's embrace, though it did not take away her pain and guilt.

"I told Mr Fletcher of the investments," she said.

"Louisa-Margaretta thought it safer not to, but I believed I had no choice."

Morgan kissed her through his laughter. Another man might have taken advantage of Judith's heightened emotion and the relative privacy of their situation to seek more embraces, but Morgan must have known she was in no fit state for romance. Instead, he led her to a chair and sat very close to her, holding her hands as she tried to regain her composure.

"It matters not at all, Judith," he said. "I'm surprised if he pretended to be ignorant, though I suppose it is like him. I had already told him, and I'm sure Mr Haddington must have mentioned it as well."

Judith sighed. That knowledge unlocked some of the tightness in her throat, and she breathed again.

"He said nothing of that," she said. "Perhaps he is more devious than I thought."

"Whatever his character," said Morgan, "you were right to tell him. I hope he gave you credit for that."

Judith shook her head. "He did not seem to have sympathy for any of us. To own the truth, he seemed rather superior about being called out to Wycliff Castle again. He didn't say anything directly, but he implied that guests here were not ever safe."

Morgan sighed, letting go of one of Judith's hands and tracing the other with his finger.

"That will never stand up in a court of law," he said, and Judith felt relieved enough to be able to feel, once again, affection for her beloved.

But with that rush of love came fear. "We should marry now," she said. "If we are married, we will be together no matter what he chooses to do."

Morgan raised his eyebrows. "You do not think that he

will have me hauled away, simply because Mr Lush stole my watch?"

"I do not know what to think," said Judith, her voice even. With her resolution came a sort of calm, though she knew Mr Fletcher's power and prejudices could easily bring Morgan to a very bad end.

"Even if he does," said Morgan, "I am sure that the Haddingtons would provide me with every legal remedy. In that sense, we are both fortunate to be connected to this family."

"All that might not protect you," insisted Judith.

"But marriage to a pauper would not protect *you*," said Morgan. "I know we are both devoted to a plain way of life, but I cannot leave you penniless."

Judith pulled her hand away, staring at Morgan. "So I ought to go through this castle myself, looking for your father's watch? Otherwise, you'll abandon your promise?"

"Of course not," he said. "But I must have something for us to live on before we marry. That is all."

Judith rose to her feet. "If we are to marry soon, the only thing for it is finding that watch."

29

Judith had spent only half an hour looking for the watch before she discovered that her quest was pointless. Mr Lush's room was locked, and none of the other rooms where she looked seemed to have a hidden compartment. She would do better, she decided, if she found Morgan a profession and gave up on the watch. And there was one person in the household who was exceedingly good at finding positions for others.

One person, of course, who hated Judith. But she had to hope that Mrs Haddington's affection for Morgan, her own blood relative, would win out.

Judith was almost relieved to learn that Mrs Haddington was no longer at home. But before she could lose her nerve, Judith resolved to look for her hostess in all of the grand lady's favourite haunts.

Just because Mrs Haddington had gone out, there was no reason to believe she would be walking the grounds. In fact, it was much more likely that she had gone to the village, perhaps to share news or commiserate with some of the people whom she imagined were fond of her visits. Mrs

Haddington had never yet learned that her wealth and position meant that others deferred to her, even to the point of pretending pleasure when she dropped by unannounced. Though Louisa-Margaretta said often enough, "Of course they would admit you, Mama. They could hardly refuse, after all," Mrs Haddington was simply too pleased with her own generous, God-fearing ways to admit the possibility that some of the recipients of her charity might prefer privacy to conversation. But even those young people were in a better position than Judith, who dreaded the idea of confronting Mrs Haddington. Still, Morgan was Mrs Haddington's blood relative, and that was the only quarter from which they might reasonably expect help.

In the past week, Judith had begun to be angry at Mrs Haddington for resenting her. For years, Judith had stood by Louisa-Margaretta, whose many rash decisions and moral transgressions would have shocked even her mother had they become generally known. But instead of working to help her struggling daughter, Mrs Haddington insisted on blaming Judith for all the turmoil. Once Judith was sure that she could marry Morgan, leave Derbyshire forever, and escape Mrs Haddington's wrath, she felt she could bear it. But trapped near Wycliff Castle as she was, the nature of the situation acted like a cage on Judith's heart.

It was high time she took every step she could, however desperate, to solve the problem.

The Haddingtons' gardens were neat enough in winter, though Judith found that she missed the flowers of spring. Though she might never see the grounds again once she left, the memory of that first spring with Morgan would always remain with her. There was no lovelier place to fall in love. Even in winter, the tall hedges and bare trees were rather romantic.

A seldom-used bridge and a folly sat at the end of the garden, and Judith decided to check them for the lady of the house, though she knew that to be a fool's errand. She could spend a few more moments recalling the sweetness of her courtship before she took steps to prepare herself for a hasty marriage, one that would be small and rushed due to her fear of the gallows.

It appeared that Judith was not the only person who found the garden romantic. It was a place with an excellent amount of privacy for a courting couple, and others had certainly become aware of that fact.

For as soon as Judith entered the folly, she found Miss Blackmore and Miss Guppy together, locked into an embrace that was plainly not conducive to a romantic but chaste friendship.

30

"I'm very sorry, I would prefer to ride alone," said Louisa-Margaretta, much gratified by the surprise in Mr Blackmore's eyes.

They were outside, near the stables. Louisa-Margaretta knew that she looked well in her riding habit, and she was gratified that her mother had insisted on having a new one made for her on their last visit to a London dressmaker. True, Mrs Haddington had intended the riding habit to be part of a trousseau, something Louisa-Margaretta could wear to enchant her new husband and impress any acquaintances she might make as a married woman.

Fortunately, even without any social engagements, Louisa-Margaretta was still able to make use of the garments. They would be both stylish and comfortable while she was riding, which was good enough. If she happened to look perfectly lovely while Mr Blackmore begged for the privilege of accompanying her, well, that was also most convenient.

"I had thought you might appreciate my company, after our conversation," said Mr Blackmore, plainly confused that his invitation to accompany the lovely Miss Haddington had been rescinded.

"Which conversation was that?" asked Louisa-Margaretta, her tone perfectly pleasant. "The one at dinner yesterday, where you ignored me then stormed away from my mother's table?"

"I have offended you," he said. "I offend everyone."

It was not an apology, and Louisa-Margaretta was not inclined to treat it as such.

"Yes, well, I am sure that is your misfortune." She nodded to one of the grooms. They knew which horse to bring her, and she did not have to ask anymore.

"Yes, it is," he said, plainly puzzled. "I give offense even when I do not mean to. And I was so distressed by the things that Mr Ramsbury was saying, I'm afraid—"

Louisa-Margaretta walked over to Godiva, tired of Mr Blackmore's excuses. She herself did not like to apologise, but the man was making himself ridiculous.

"Mr Ramsbury is my cousin," she said shortly. "If you would like to seek his pardon, by all means do so, but you shouldn't try to make any apologies through me."

Mr Blackmore stopped as if surprised. Louisa-Margaretta knew, rather wickedly, that he had not been at all interested in begging Cousin Morgan's pardon. But it was rather fun to pretend that she thought he was ready to repent of those insults.

"I am really a very good rider," he offered.

"I am sure you are," said Louisa-Margaretta. "Another day, we shall ride together."

He did look quite handsome in his riding clothes. His dark features, almost as becoming as his sister's, looked as if they belonged in the moody Derbyshire landscape. Clouds were gathering, the weak sunlight making his skin look particularly gorgeous, and Louisa-Margaretta thought about how much she would love to steal another kiss from the man.

If, that was, he behaved himself. And if he were suitably punished.

"I hope you have an excellent afternoon, Mr Blackmore," said Louisa-Margaretta over her shoulder. "Though if I were you, I would hurry indoors. It looks like it may snow very soon."

A little weather would not stop her. But she enjoyed implying that Mr Blackmore was the sort of young man who would melt if he stayed out of doors too long.

She believed his boast about his skill at riding, but she knew that it was something he would need to show off later.

31

Miss Guppy had her hands over her face. Judith saw that the young woman was beginning to weep. Miss Blackmore looked defiant but perplexed.

"Miss St Clair," she said, but she appeared unable to say anything else.

"Miss Guppy, Miss Blackmore," said Judith, catching her breath. "Have you seen Mrs Haddington?"

Miss Guppy started weeping more, and Judith went over to where the young woman was seated on a bench.

"Please," she said. "I did not mean to distress you—"

"Don't touch her," snapped Miss Blackmore. "I don't know what you think you saw, Miss St Clair —"

"Nothing!" said Judith hastily. "I would never gossip about any detail of a private meeting, I assure you."

Miss Blackmore appeared skeptical, as well she might. "You'll forgive me, Miss St Clair. But I cannot trust you to keep your word."

Miss Guppy finally lowered her hands. "Of course she

will not keep it secret. What a notion! My parents will separate us forever."

At that, she clung to Miss Blackmore, and Judith nearly laughed.

"You can trust me," she said. "Please, do not distress yourself."

"You told that magistrate that Mr Lush was a swindler," hissed Miss Blackmore. "Now the magistrate suspects my brother!"

Judith sighed. "He suspects my own fiancé. Yet you understand why I had to tell him. What are the chances he never would have learned of this on his own? Better for him to know immediately."

"Exactly," said Miss Guppy, glaring at her. "You do not keep any secrets. We cannot possibly trust you."

Judith tried not to grimace. It was rather a pointless discussion, at the heart of it. Even if she were going to say something, there would be nothing the two ladies could do to stop her. Still, she could not help chiding them.

"Anyone might have come here," she said. "But because it was only I, the two of you must be more careful in the future."

Miss Blackmore scoffed. "You're one to lecture us, then. Where exactly do you propose we go? We neither of us have any money of our own."

"Perhaps Paris," said Judith quietly.

"Paris?" said Miss Guppy. "Without money, did you hear her?"

"You'd have to get husbands, of course," said Judith.

Miss Guppy stood to go. "You're just like the rest of them. I'm not going to go look for a husband, never!"

But Miss Blackmore appeared interested in Judith's plan, though skeptical. "They would find us out eventually. You did, after all, and we've only been in the same household for a matter of days."

Miss Guppy stood in the doorway, glaring at them.

"First of all," said Judith, "I have some skill and experience in discovering others' secrets, though in this instance, I can assure you it was simply a matter of luck. Secondly, I was not speaking of genuine marriages. You need husbands whom you can trust absolutely, and there is only one manner of man who would not make demands on you."

Miss Guppy frowned. "A very poor man? That's your idea, then, that we go to the continent with fortune hunters?"

Judith blushed. Her cousin Jasper, who was deeply immersed in the theatrical world, was able to speak of such matters more easily than she. But she endeavored to explain as explicitly as she could.

"It would have to be a very peculiar arrangement," she said, though privately, she thought that marriages free of affection or understanding were not at all uncommon. Louisa-Margaretta's parents always seemed to be an exception to the general tendency.

"Peculiar indeed," said Miss Blackmore, "and probably not possible. Come, Miss St Clair, you are about to be married yourself. Can you imagine a husband who would not pressure you to give him an heir? It is unheard of."

Judith looked at them firmly. "My friends would not, to give you one example. The gentlemen you already know of, the Duke of Ormonde and his companion, have no interest in marrying women. I am absolutely clear on this point. You may ask Louisa-Margaretta if you do not believe me. She can confirm every particular of our acquaintance."

Miss Guppy blushed. "I do not know such men.

Certainly not on terms where I could ever suggest such a thing."

But Miss Blackmore was thoughtful. "I might have a gentleman or two I could call on," she mused.

After having visited London's most important literary salons, Judith was fairly sure that Miss Blackmore had more than one gentleman friend who was, at least outwardly, rather fond of his bachelor status.

"You cannot marry in haste," said Judith. "Even if your marriage is not, well, what one might refer to as traditional, you still put yourself in the legal and physical power of a man as soon as the vows are spoken."

Miss Blackmore blinked. "As we are well aware. You sound almost as if you do not believe in the institution yourself, Miss St Clair."

Judith hesitated. That was quite a challenge to her feelings for Morgan, but she had to admit there was plenty of truth in the words.

"Marriage is not what it ought to be," she said finally. "Not economically or spiritually. As Quakers, we believe that a marriage binds two worthy individuals before a community, but I'm afraid that societally, it is little better than a tool to bludgeon women into obedient silence."

Miss Blackmore actually laughed. Though Miss Guppy still skulked in the doorway, Judith could see that Miss Blackmore, at least, finally believed she was not a threat.

"Judith St Clair, I never took you for such a radical," she said, putting an arm through Judith's. Miss Guppy's angry scowl was unmistakable, though as they left the folly, Miss Blackmore took her lover's arm as well.

"My views ought not to be radical," said Judith, "though I'm afraid they are uncommon. Anyway, it is of little importance. I came here to ask Mrs Haddington to help me gain my father's permission to marry, and I'm afraid I still must seek her out."

"Let us go back to the house together, then," said Miss Blackmore. "Now that we are assured of your discretion, perhaps you can help us and say that we all went out walking together."

"I should be quite happy to do so," said Judith, though a knot of dread formed in her stomach. As long as she was arm in arm with Miss Blackmore, listening to the young woman cajole Miss Guppy into good spirits again, she was safe.

Once she entered the castle, she might very well have to do battle.

32

Judith stood silently outside the sitting room next to Mrs Haddington's bedroom. If she was perfectly still, she would not be discovered or announced, and she might never have to face the lady of the house.

Not for the first time, she wondered about her plan. Mrs Haddington knew that Morgan was looking for work, and she had probably offered to help more than once.

But Morgan, though he fought any semblance of pride, had been raised not to depend on his relatives. He probably would have demurred or perhaps told her that he would not be content to work in many occupations open to him. The military occupations, certainly, were too violent for his religious beliefs. His brief turn as a diplomat had been disastrous, he had no interest in business, and his Quaker path made him unfit to be a clergyman. He could be some sort of Quaker leader, certainly, but the emphasis on equality inherent in the religion did not lend itself to lucrative positions.

Judith could put it to Mrs Haddington much more plainly. Morgan must have some work, and with her extensive connections, she was extremely well placed to find such a thing for him. Judith hoped that Mrs Haddington's contempt for her would not interfere with her altruistic impulses.

Before Judith could announce herself, one of the maids came running up.

"I beg your pardon, Miss St Clair," said Harriet. "I've a message for my mistress."

Judith stood back, and Harriet went in. Judith could just hear the young woman saying something about a far corner of the estate.

"Poachers," said Mrs Haddington. "Well, there's nothing for it. Go find all the men you can. I'll direct them."

Judith rushed off, secretly glad that the poachers had prevented her from speaking to Mrs Haddington. Perhaps, if she waited another day, a miracle would take place and Morgan would hear favourably about some position or another.

It would truly have to be a miracle. But if nothing else, she could pray.

33

After her ride, Louisa-Margaretta entered Wycliff Castle feeling refreshed. At least Christmas in Derbyshire wouldn't be completely miserable, provided she could go out on Godiva every day. Finally, for the first time since her broken engagement, she was beginning to feel all the benefits of spinsterhood. To be sure, she was dependent on her parents, but apart from trying to interfere with her marriage prospects, they were unlikely to do her harm. She lived in a comfortable home, one which entailed virtually no responsibilities, and she could ride whenever she wished.

She could even entertain herself by flirting with visitors such as Mr Blackmore, provided she chose the right sort of man. A smile came to her instantly when she thought of his surprise on learning that she didn't wish to ride with him any longer. With men whom she genuinely loved, such as Isaac, Louisa-Margaretta thought such coquettish games unspeakably foolish. But now that Mr Blackmore had been chastened into trying once again to win her over, he might suppress his poor manners. That was really the most one could hope for from a man of his sort.

As Louisa-Margaretta entered the main hall, ready to ascend the grand staircase and change into one of her loveliest gowns, she saw Mr Blackmore conferring with her mother.

"Miss Haddington," he said, and she was pleased to note that he appeared even more deferential than before. "Is there any chance your horse is not yet unsaddled?"

"Surely not, Mr Blackmore," said Mrs Haddington sharply. "My daughter will not be going."

The young man shook his head. "I did not mean Miss Haddington might ride out, of course. But I myself could go."

"Go where?" asked Louisa-Margaretta, and her mother's face fell.

"One of the groundkeepers reported some suspicious activity on the west side of the lake, near that little clearing with the spring," said Mrs Haddington. "But the men are going, Louisa-Margaretta. Mr Blackmore, you are more than welcome to join them. My daughter, of course, will stay here."

Louisa-Margaretta actually laughed. "Of course I shan't stay, Mama. Come, Mr Blackmore. They can get fresh horses for both of us. It will only take a moment."

"All of the servants are out looking," insisted Mrs Haddington, but Louisa-Margaretta only grinned.

"I'm better at finding things than they are, Mama," she said. "Also, I am already dressed. And though my dear Godiva may be too tired, I am sure they shall find some horse for me that is suitably rested."

Mr Guppy hurried across. "I heard something about

men in the woods. Surely you are not thinking of going after them yourself, Miss Haddington?"

Mrs Haddington glared at her daughter. "I could not keep her indoors," she said, her voice rich with disapproval. "You have said you are a skilled rider, Mr Blackmore. Can you protect my daughter?"

"Of course, ma'am," he said.

Mr Guppy looked surprised, but he made no comment.

"Very well," said Mrs Haddington. "Go find your horses, but wait for my orders. Everyone is going, and I don't want you to arrive before the men who are going on foot."

"That is rather the purpose of taking a horse," grumbled Louisa-Margaretta.

By the time she and Mr Blackmore reached the stables, Louisa-Margaretta had cheerfully decided to disobey her mother's instructions. It took a great deal of time for suitable horses to be found and prepared, and while they waited, a large party of men and women set off from Wycliff Castle. Louisa-Margaretta noticed Judith sneak off after them, and she suppressed a smile. Judith fighting poachers, what a thought! If the group moved quietly, she supposed it was just possible they might surprise the brutes. More likely, they would find nothing. At least Louisa-Margaretta, if provided with a good horse, might have a chance.

"We may as well go," she said, and when Mr Blackmore hesitated, she gave him a winning smile.

"I am not afraid of Mama," said Louisa-Margaretta. "You are more than welcome to stay behind, Mr Blackmore, but then you shall have to explain to her why you let me ride off alone."

As soon as their ride began, Louisa-Margaretta knew that it might be in vain. For reasons of her own, she did not want to have to share her time with Mr Blackmore. If they followed the party that had set out on foot, they would reach the clearing quickly, but they would be under the scrutiny of that large party if they did so.

If Louisa-Margaretta took Mr Blackmore on a longer route, up through the hills and then down into the ravine, she would have him all to herself. So she did so.

At first, it was rather thrilling, riding through the darkening woods with a handsome man who plainly desired her. Louisa-Margaretta had to slow her pace slightly to accommodate Mr Blackmore, who was nearly breathless when he spoke.

"You know these woods well," he said as their horses struggled up a rocky slope. "I should dearly love to see more of them."

"I should dearly love to show you more of them," said Louisa-Margaretta. "Do you ride often?"

"I haven't been able to recently," he said. "Nancy isn't a great rider. I'm sure few women are as quick or as brave as you, Miss Haddington."

Though he plainly meant it as a compliment, Louisa-Margaretta soured a bit at the mention of Mr Blackmore's absent wife. The less she thought about the bedridden Mrs Blackmore, the better.

"I am not so very brave," she said. "I just love riding."

"No, you are extraordinary," he said, just as their horses reached a part of the ride that was relatively even.

"Am I?" said Louisa-Margaretta, grinning. "Well, if you think I am, I suppose I shall have to prove it."

And she spurred her horse on, moving faster down the path. Mr Blackmore kept up, at least at first. They had to slow somewhat as the terrain sloped down toward a little stream, but Louisa-Margaretta didn't find the going difficult.

"This is terribly rocky," said Mr Blackmore. "Miss Haddington, if you could slow your horse down just a bit."

She pretended not to hear. Soon the ground would be more even. They were near the spring that her mother had spoken of. It was odd that the groundskeeper had not simply confronted any poachers himself, but perhaps he was afraid of being outnumbered. Since Mrs Haddington refused to hear of employing a gamekeeper to catch poachers, they had to call on a rather ad hoc assortment of Wycliff Castle men each time such activity was suspected. Louisa-Margaretta saw the clearing, particularly bare in the winter, where the spring burbled up when it was not frozen.

And that was where Louisa-Margaretta saw what she had been seeking—a little flash of cloth in the trees, the sight of a nearly bare arm clutching an animal in a trap.

It was strange that she had compared Mr Blackmore's romantic pursuit of her to a hunt. Louisa-Margaretta, who loved genuine hunts, knew that the thrill was unmistakable, much more dramatic than pursuing some pretty lady in a ballroom. Spurring her horse on, she went faster, straining to catch a glimpse of the person.

She'd arrived before any of the men from Wycliff Castle, of course, so they were alone. Louisa-Margaretta had just moments to see the person's face before he would surely disappear, and that would mean jumping her horse over the stream. Godiva could have done it, she knew, but the stout bay they had given her might not be able to make it. Louisa-Margaretta, who had maintained the sidesaddle position required of a lady throughout, swung one leg over her horse so she was sitting astride it like a man. The saddle was not meant for that position, but it was the safest way.

They sailed over the stream in a perfect leap, just in time for Louisa-Margaretta to see a young girl's face whiten in surprise and terror. Then the young lady, still clutching her dead pheasant in its trap, turned and ran.

The young girl's face was not unfamiliar. Though Louisa-Margaretta seldom concerned herself with the names of various visitors, she knew where the girl lived. The family was very poor.

Sighing, Louisa-Margaretta stopped her horse, who stomped and panted from the exertion. She had to wait for Mr Blackmore, who was charging toward the creek faster than he could quite manage.

Louisa-Margaretta could have called out to him. Instead, she simply shook her head then raised a finger in front of her to warn him off crossing the stream as she had.

He insisted on jumping it. And unlike Louisa-Margaretta, he was not at all successful.

At least the horse was uninjured, thought Louisa-Margaretta, sliding off her own horse and running to the man where he had fallen.

For a moment, she went to where he lay and felt as if she were a goddess of the forest. He was breathing heavily, and when Louisa-Margaretta leaned over him, he pulled her head down and kissed her. But the embrace lasted only a moment before he broke it off, crying out in pain.

Louisa-Margaretta, shocked, sat up, staring at Mr Blackmore. And that was when she saw his leg.

It was broken. It looked so unnatural, the angle of the lower bone not quite right, that a bloodier wound would have been much easier to bear.

Immediately, she felt ill, though Mr Blackmore did not seem to notice at all.

"Oh, Miss Haddington," he said. "You are a much better rider than I am. I could not keep up, only I did not wish to slow you down, and you are so beautiful—"

Louisa-Margaretta moved farther from him, hoping she would not ever have to see his leg again. She felt as if she could easily vomit into the bushes. Instead, she forced herself to take very deep breaths then touched a series of points on her face and wrists. It was a technique she had learned in the asylum, and though she would never admit to any tendency toward madness or melancholy in herself, it was rather helpful at such moments.

The terrain was treacherous, but the party who had followed on foot were able to follow the stream without any great difficulty. Since Mr Blackmore had fallen at the low point of the ravine, the whole party traipsed over in response to Louisa-Margaretta's whistle.

Her papa was first to encounter them. He leaned down, shaking his head, and took a good look at Mr Blackmore's leg while Louisa-Margaretta stayed well out of the way.

"It's going to hurt like the devil," said Mr Haddington.

"Here," said Judith.

Louisa-Margaretta peered at her friend, who was on her knees next to Mr Blackmore. Though Judith might well break her heart over any number of silly things, she was very good with the sick and the dying. And the dead, in fact. Louisa-Margaretta could never get used to the horror of seeing a dead person's face, whereas Judith always simply dropped to her knees in prayer. It came of being a clergyman's daughter, apparently. Judith had been nearby when any number of people breathed their last, whereas Louisa-Margaretta disliked illness as a general rule and would do almost anything to avoid invalids.

"We must bind it to a stick," said Judith. "It will still be painful, I'm afraid, but if we can at least get it stable, that will make the journey back a bit easier."

"Yes," said Cousin Morgan, who gently touched his

fiancée's hand before rising to his feet and looking about the darkening woods. "Let me see what I can find."

Louisa-Margaretta went over to her horse. She quickly found her father, marking him as the person least likely to take offense at her departure.

"Papa," she said, surprised to see tears forming in his eyes. "What is it?"

"Nothing," he said. "Only your cousin and your... your friend, they are natural healers, I think."

Louisa-Margaretta snorted. Her father could be harsh in his business decisions, she knew, so it was even more silly to see him getting sentimental over the concerted efforts of an engaged couple. Perhaps he was the one who would help Cousin Morgan find work.

"If you like them so much, you ought to find a position for Cousin Morgan," she said. "Then they could marry, and Judith would get her dowry."

Her father frowned. "It's not my place. And he didn't want to work for me, last I asked."

"When did you last ask him?"

"Earlier today," her father said quietly.

Louisa-Margaretta rolled her eyes. Of course her father would do everything to make things smooth for a young cousin who wasn't even his blood relative. Meanwhile, he had been all too happy to break his daughter's engagement into pieces.

"Well, I'm going back," she said. "And Papa, honestly, you can't object to my going alone. If Mr Blackmore hadn't been with me, I would have caught the men by now."

"You didn't happen to get a look at them, did you?"

"No," Louisa-Margaretta lied. She doubted that either of her parents would want to punish the little girl for poaching, but the child was probably scared off it forever in any case. There was no sense in throwing her name into anyone's mind, especially when Louisa-Margaretta always thought she herself would've made an excellent thief.

"Very well, Lou," he said. "But be careful."

She grinned, trying not to think about Mr Blackmore's leg. "I am always careful, Papa."

34

Judith was tasked with speaking to Mr Blackmore. There were more than enough strong men to lift him, and they did so. They had even managed to bind both his legs to a coat placed on the underside of his horse's saddle so that he would not be jostled as much on the trek to Wycliff Castle. Even then, his face was changing colour with the pain, and he moaned as much as he spoke.

"Oh," he cried as they went along one rocky path. "Stop, lay me down. Give me one moment's rest."

Judith kept close to the man, nodding in sympathy. "I believe I heard Mrs Blackmore say something very similar recently."

Mr Blackmore, even in pain, scoffed. "She is bearing a child. All women do it."

"And all women endure pain," said Judith. "Some at the beginning, all at the end, and many all the way through."

"Not this pain," maintained Mr Blackmore, but Judith began quoting from the Old Testament. The words came easily to her. When one's family read from the Scriptures every evening, the words were unforgettable.

"'Unto the woman he said, I will greatly multiply thy sorrow and thy conception; in sorrow thou shalt bring forth children,'" said Judith.

She did not repeat the next part of God's curse, though she remembered it perfectly: "'And thy desire shall be to thy husband, and he shall rule over thee.'"

The second part, indeed, was a curse! She thought of poor Mrs Blackmore, bedridden and in pain, with only her mother and Mrs Crampton offering any sympathy. Mr Blackmore might be ruling over his wife, but that was surely harmful to both of them. He had never expressed any genuine concern for her suffering, and Judith wondered if his current state would inspire him at all to seek her forgiveness.

"Mrs Crampton knew pain," said Mr Blackmore, and Judith turned her head in concern. She was fairly sure that the other men carrying him heard little of what he was saying, but she lowered her voice in case they listened.

"Do not think of Mrs Crampton," she said, worried that he was growing delirious. "Only rest, and we shall help you as much as we can."

Then Mr Blackmore's voice grew weak, and Judith had to stand near him, stumbling over the rocks and branches in the path as she did so.

"Mrs Crampton's own son was taken in," he said. "It was Mr Lush. A bad investment, and he took his own life. She told me—good money after bad."

Judith stopped on the path for a moment, and she had to rush to keep up with the party of gentlemen.

"You are not to blame," she said loudly enough for

everyone to hear. After all, she could be speaking of the accident or of anything else. It was best that nobody else knew the secret about Mrs Crampton, at least not until Judith had decided what it meant.

"I am to blame," he said. "She tried to help me, but I was too proud."

Judith could only hope the men thought he was speaking of Louisa-Margaretta. Those words would have applied to her, at least somewhat. But Louisa-Margaretta, as far as Judith could tell, had done very little to help except alert the rescuers to Mr Blackmore's position. She did not stay with him and, as soon as Judith arrived, was happy to get on her horse and ride off.

"You have not been too proud," said Judith, hoping to keep all skepticism out of her tone. Indeed, Mr Blackmore was very proud, but when he was writhing in pain, she thought it best not to mention that.

"I can only blame myself," said Mr Blackmore. "I was foolish."

"Hush," said Judith. "Save your strength."

She knew that even if someone could do a good job of setting Mr Blackmore's leg, the healing process itself would be very long and painful.

As they came within sight of Wycliff Castle, Judith fell back. Since she could not set the leg herself, there would be little need for her assistance. The Haddingtons had an army of servants who could come with cold compresses, and no doubt Mrs Crampton would be about with healing draughts.

The only trouble was, Judith was not at all sure that that was safe. *Should a woman who had killed one of their houseguests be entrusted with healing the sick?* But it would be odd to try to have the old woman barred without a reason.

Judith sighed. She needed Louisa-Margaretta's advice on that point, and quickly. Otherwise, in spite of his current predicament, Mr Blackmore might come to even greater harm.

As soon as Louisa-Margaretta reached Wycliff Castle, she realised that she was starving. Knowing that those who had not joined the search party would have provided food, she went to the breakfast room, where she was gratified to find a warm fire and a considerable spread. Apparently, that was to be their dinner, and the informality suited her. Judith came in when she was eating some bread and cold meat, having warmed herself by the fire and touched up her appearance with the aid of a mirror.

But when Judith relayed what Mr Blackmore had said of Mrs Crampton, Louisa-Margaretta was too shocked to keep eating.

"Are you quite sure?" she asked. "I mean, we thought it might be a woman, but an ancient woman?"

"Mrs Crampton is hardly ancient," said Judith. "I believe the loss of her son affected her deeply. And as you have seen yourself, she is quite competent."

Louisa-Margaretta sighed. "Well, leave it, then. Mr Fletcher has not had anyone arrested, so I suppose that is a good sign. As long as it doesn't mean that an innocent man goes to the gallows, we can refrain from speaking about the old woman."

"You're right," said Judith. "Sending her to prison, given her age, would be tantamount to a death sentence."

"Oh, I have no worries on that score," said Louisa-Margaretta airily. "I suppose she may very well deserve it, given what she did to Mr Lush. But you know that it would cause the most terrible scandal."

"You are very worried about scandal, then," said Judith.

Louisa-Margaretta shrugged. "I cannot pretend that my family's reputation is unblemished. But it would be rather convenient for us to hang on to whatever honour we have left, yes. Who knows but that one of us may need it someday."

Judith was silent as Louisa-Margaretta continued eating.

"If that is all, I suppose you can go home, Judith," said Louisa-Margaretta. A quick glance at her friend told her that all the walking in the dark had not done her coiffure or her complexion any favours, and Judith liked to rest early.

Judith would not leave. Louisa-Margaretta looked at her.

"Why did you take Mr Blackmore with you?" asked Judith. "He is not as strong a rider as you are. Indeed, very few people are."

Louisa-Margaretta smiled. "Oh, I am well aware of that, Judith. But Mama would not have let me go without some companion, and he has been begging to ride with me for some days."

"And you have been encouraging him," said Judith.

Louisa-Margaretta scoffed. "This is most unlike you, Judith," she said severely. "Whatever happened to your belief that the person who made the wedding vows is most to blame for any bending of those vows?"

"Bending," said Judith.

Louisa-Margaretta did not answer. She took another bite of her meat instead, though the flavour seemed to have gone off a bit.

"I do believe that," said Judith, "especially as concerns men who are married. But, Louisa-Margaretta, my mother always told me that this does not fully absolve the woman. One should never enter into such a situation. It puts the wife into an unfortunate position, and nobody involved is blameless."

Louisa-Margaretta did not pretend to have any patience with Judith's proselytizing. "I can hardly argue with your mother, Judith. But you needn't worry about me. Mr Blackmore is nothing more than a temporary Christmas amusement, the same as snapdragon or bullet pudding. When the holiday ends, he shall return with his wife, and it will all be forgot."

"Will it?" said Judith, and Louisa-Margaretta knew her friend's thoughts. They only angered her.

"I am not an idiot," she said. "I know how to be cautious."

Though she did wonder. If she achieved her aim of finding a moment with an unattended and adoring Mr Blackmore, her every effort at restraint might well betray her.

"It is not what you truly desire, though," said Judith. "Please, Louisa-Margaretta, we both know this. You have been unsettled ever since that mention of Mr Rod—"

"That's quite enough," said Louisa-Margaretta. "I am the one who found the place where the poachers were."

"Poachers?" said Judith. "Is that what happened?"

Louisa-Margaretta considered telling her friend about the young girl. Certainly, she had always intended to tell Judith. But she had no intention of staying in the room, getting a lecture from a condescending woman whose spotless virtue and long engagement seemed to give her some sort of upper hand.

"You may leave," said Louisa-Margaretta. "And don't come back in the morning either. I will speak to the old lady, and now that everything is solved, you have no reason to visit before the new year."

Judith's face fell. "Louisa-Margaretta, please. It is only because of my regard for you—"

"That you order me around as if you were my grandmother? No, thank you very much, Judith. I have had quite enough of your sermons for one evening. You may go now."

35

Judith could no longer depend on her friendship with Louisa-Margaretta, but neither could she leave Wycliff Castle with the identity of the killer a secret. She sought Morgan, which was not difficult. He was waiting in the library for her. It was the place they both frequented in bad weather, but Judith had long ago convinced herself that it was not improper of them to do so if they never made a fixed plan to meet there. Morgan seemed to understand that.

"I have had an idea," he said, rising to greet her as soon as she came in. "It is about your brother."

Judith sighed, sinking down on the sofa where Morgan had been sitting. It felt like her day had lasted an age already.

"I am glad you are thinking of Joseph," she said, endeavoring to use patience. "But I must speak to you about Mr Lush."

He shook his head, sitting next to her, rather close but without touching her. "In many ways, it is a good thing that our marriage has been delayed. It will give you an opportunity to put your brother's fears to rest."

"His fears," said Judith slowly.

"Yes," said Morgan. "He is terrified that you will abandon him. I'm sure he sees all of your absences as abandonment, though I know very well how much Louisa-Margaretta has depended on you."

Judith sighed. At least there was one relative of Louisa-Margaretta who seemed to understand the nature of their friendship. To Mrs Haddington, Judith was always a hindrance, never a help. To Mr Haddington, well, she could not say. He had clearly not spoken up to challenge his wife's behavior, although Judith also noted that everything Mrs Haddington said and did in front of her husband was calculated and correct. Her smiles, in his sight, were a little bit warmer, and she even occasionally used "Judith" instead of the frosty "Miss St Clair." Perhaps that was an indicator that Mr Haddington thought better of Judith than his wife did, although it would be impossible to tell.

"You think that I ought to stay with Joseph, then?" Judith tried to fight back her emotions. "Are you so certain that we will never find your watch?"

"No." Morgan took her hands in his. "I am not at all worried about that. Of course we will marry, but if your brother believes he will never see you again, I am sure that will be most troubling for him."

Judith looked quickly over her shoulder at the door then allowed herself to lean into Morgan's embrace.

"Thank you for thinking of him," she said sincerely. "I'm afraid I have quite forgotten him these last few days, I have been so worried for you."

"I am sure that is exactly what he was afraid of," said Morgan, gently stroking Judith's thin hair. It had gotten quite messy during the rush through the woods. "He needs to know that you will always be his sister."

Judith swallowed. "I will tell him," she said solemnly. "One of the servants can see me home tonight."

"I would rather see you home," said Morgan, holding her closer, but Judith shook her head.

"You must stay. Louisa-Margaretta and I have discovered the identity of the killer."

As she had predicted, that put every amorous thought out of Morgan's head. "And you think we are in danger? Who is it?"

"I am fairly sure we are not in danger," she said. "But there is a great deal more to Mrs Crampton than we suspected."

Morgan's gasp was audible. "She was working with Mr Lush! Judith, I did not wish to slander her, but I knew there was something wrong with her presence here. That she would wish to spend Christmas with such an unpleasant family, even if she received some payment in return! I could never account for her presence."

Judith winced at the description, but she could not contradict it. The Guppy and Blackmore families, apart from the secret romance between the two unmarried daughters, were almost all at odds. She wondered if there was some sort of *Romeo and Juliet* element that had driven Miss Guppy and Miss Blackmore together against all the animosity between the two married couples.

"She was not working with Mr Lush," said Judith firmly. "She was working against him. Well, she was trying to, but ultimately, she must have found that she could not convince any of the men to resist his scheme. Mrs Crampton's son, you see, was taken in and ended up taking his own life."

"And so she harmed Mr Lush in cold blood?" Morgan

seemed incredulous. "Even as an act of revenge, it is scarcely believable."

Judith shook her head. "I believe that she must have been defending herself. For even if she sought him out, if he attacked her, what would she have at hand? Only something from her workbasket. I do not think that such an elderly woman would go speak with a young, strong gentleman, all the while planning to overpower him physically."

There was silence, then Judith added, "I do plan to ask her, of course. But tomorrow, when it is light."

"If she is blackmailing others, she is still a danger," said Morgan.

Judith wondered if she ought to tell him about Miss Guppy and Miss Blackmore. Though she knew that Morgan would not be unkind, she realised that she could not trust him with that secret. Perhaps if Miss Guppy and Miss Blackmore managed to marry respectable men and move to Paris, it would be safer to share such things. But for the moment, Judith had to respect their privacy.

"I do not believe she was using her knowledge for personal gain," said Judith. "But if she was trying to warn Mr Lush off, at the same time keeping men like Mr Blackmore away, she must have eventually seen that this could not work."

Morgan held her close, and briefly, Judith was tempted to stay at Wycliff Castle. How easy it would be to take advantage of the general confusion and steal some time with her beloved in the winter darkness!

But she could not forget her duty to her family, and she would need to be well rested if she and Louisa-Margaretta were to confront the old woman.

"Good night, my love," she said, and Morgan reluctantly relinquished her.

"Be careful," he said, and she nodded.

"Look after everyone," said Judith. "If I am wrong, I am worried that something may happen tonight."

36

After her conversation with Judith, Louisa-Margaretta smarted with shame for a quarter of an hour. She could not stand her friend's accusations. Nor could she, with a very clear conscience, evaluate her own actions. Of course she had been flirting with Mr Blackmore! Though he needed little encouragement in the end. And as soon as he hurt his leg, Louisa-Margaretta was quite sure that he would have done anything for her.

In her room, she did not prepare herself for sleep. Instead, she put on a housedress. If she was rather more attentive to her appearance than one might expect, given that the hour was late and she would likely not encounter anyone on her trip through the great mansion's passageways, nobody could fault her for that.

She cursed Judith as she made her way to Mr Blackmore's room. Judith was such an old woman about such things! Louisa-Margaretta was quite sure that if she spent a little more time with Mr Blackmore, young Mrs Blackmore was in no state to find out. Surely there would be no harm in it at all.

And, though Louisa-Margaretta knew it to be a weak argument, she needed a distraction. Wycliff Castle had been a dreadful place ever since she returned from London. All the talk was of Judith's engagement, Miriam's engagement, and those intolerable married guests. Everyone had forgotten Louisa-Margaretta. Everyone, that was, except Mr Blackmore, who was plainly captivated by her.

She did not find him alone, of course. But his leg was in a splint, there was a glass of wine next to him, and he appeared to be perfectly awake. He was reading a novel, attended only by Mrs Crampton.

"I will take over the nursing now," Louisa-Margaretta informed the old woman, trying not to betray her shock. She should probably tell Mr Blackmore not to drink any of the wine. It might very well be poisoned.

"Very well, Miss Haddington," said Mrs Crampton with a respectful smile. "Do summon me if you need anything."

"Of course," said Louisa-Margaretta. The old woman left the room, and Louisa-Margaretta turned her attention to Mr Blackmore.

"I hope you're feeling better," she said.

"I am," he informed her. "Much better, in fact. Mrs Crampton thinks my leg will heal, and I can hardly imagine a lovelier setting in which to convalesce."

"Would you like some more wine?" asked Louisa-Margaretta, settling herself in the chair directly next to Mr Blackmore's bed. As she passed the glass over, their fingers touched. She knew she ought to warn him about the possibility of poison, but she enjoyed watching him drink his wine as he stared into her eyes.

"I'm afraid I said all sorts of foolishness when I hurt my leg," he murmured. "You must forgive me, Miss Haddington."

"There is nothing to forgive," she said swiftly, taking the glass from him. It was empty. She made sure to touch his fingertips that time, and after she refilled the glass, she handed it back most deliberately. "Unless, that is, you did not mean what you said."

He blinked but did not take his eyes off her. "Oh no, it was most sincere," he assured her.

"I am glad to hear it," said Louisa-Margaretta, feeling herself brighten at the confirmation. She had been rather confident before, of course. But she was alone, sitting next to Mr Blackmore's bed, with a perfectly good reason to be there. She sat on top of the bedclothes, bent over him, and was immediately startled by a rather loud voice in the doorway.

"Miss Haddington," said the old woman. "How fortunate. I believe I have forgotten my workbasket."

Louisa-Margaretta glared as Mrs Crampton came in, slowly bent over, and picked up her worn cloth basket. If only she could have said everything she knew about the old woman and her needles! But that suspicion was not one she could voice alone. She needed Judith with her, or someone besides the invalid Mr Blackmore, who glared at Mrs Crampton with a ferocity that matched Louisa-Margaretta's.

"Come with me, Miss Haddington," said Mrs Crampton. "I will ring for someone to sit with Mr Blackmore."

She stood in the doorway until Harriet arrived. As soon as the young woman took her place, not beside the bed but in the corner, Mrs Crampton steered Louisa-Margaretta out of the room.

"Come with me to my bedchamber, my dear," said Mrs Crampton. "I would speak to you about something."

Louisa-Margaretta's heart raced.

"Miss Haddington," said Mrs Crampton simply, as soon

as she had closed the door behind them. "You must stop pursuing Mr Blackmore. His character is weak, but yours is strong, and if you cease your attentions, you will both be quite safe."

Louisa-Margaretta scoffed, keeping a careful eye on Mrs Crampton's workbasket. The woman had laid it on the little table next to her bed, but Louisa-Margaretta kept her distance. The night had been disappointing enough. She did not need to end it by getting stabbed with a needle.

"I'm sure I have no idea what you mean," she said.

"We are alone, Miss Haddington," said Mrs Crampton, sounding weary. "We can do away with any pretense."

"Good," said Louisa-Margaretta. "I'll thank you not to meddle, then."

Mrs Crampton shook her head. "I don't wish to involve anyone else here. You're entitled to your privacy. But if you are unwilling to give up Mr Blackmore, I must take measures to protect you both..."

"Mr Blackmore is not your son," she said sharply. "You need not be so eager to protect his virtue."

Mrs Crampton only frowned. "*Mr* Blackmore! I'm worried for the man's poor wife and for you. It is always women who pay the highest price, though if a man happens to be very good, he will eventually wish to take some responsibility for his natural child."

Louisa-Margaretta could no longer keep up the pretence of respecting Mrs Crampton, and she was too angry to be afraid. "You assume too much," she snapped, going quickly to the door. "Good night, Mrs Crampton."

"Your father strayed," said the old woman, and Louisa-Margaretta paused.

She turned around, forcing herself to smile, and walked

over to the bed where the old woman was sitting, rubbing her feet.

"You have no right to say such things about my father," said Louisa-Margaretta, though Mrs Crampton's outward calm disturbed her. "Besides, you could not possibly know such a thing."

"I could, dear," said Mrs Crampton. "And you should believe me, for I'm quite sure you don't wish to know anything more about it."

"You have nothing more to say about it," said Louisa-Margaretta hotly. "And besides, it is not true." Over the years, she had seen many empty society marriages and plenty of examples of men who had made their fortunes in order to eventually marry into old, respectable families.

"I have proof," said Mrs Crampton. "But if I tell you, it will be impossible for you to ever stop yourself from knowing it."

"Oh, go on and tell me," said Louisa-Margaretta. "Besides, I don't believe it. What proof could you possibly have?"

She folded her arms across her chest as if defending herself against Mrs Crampton's answer.

But the old lady's expression made her uneasy. Even as Mrs Crampton began to speak, Louisa-Margaretta realized that she might not wish to hear any more.

But she listened.

"Miriam, wake up," Judith told her sister.

The early morning hours were the only decent time to talk. Judith knew that if she simply waited for sunrise, talking to Miriam would become impossible. Between the murder at Wycliff Castle, their three rambunctious brothers, and the presence of Mr Barnwell, the two of them were never alone.

"It's far too early," moaned Miriam, and Judith smiled.

It was a familiar refrain. She was at once happy to return to the pattern with her sister and wistful that their time together would soon come to an end, perhaps before they had mended their current disagreement. Whatever happened with Morgan, Miriam's marriage would soon take her away from the rectory forever. Whether Judith married or not, she would feel the loss.

And that, Judith had realised, was what had been troubling Joseph.

"I need your help," Judith said.

At long last, Miriam opened her eyes before immediately closing them again.

"You have to speak with Papa yourself," she said. "I've told him a thousand times he ought to relent and let you marry. He hasn't listened to Christopher or to me."

Judith's heart raced. "You spoke to Papa about my engagement? Both of you did?"

Miriam turned over and faced the wall, showing Judith only the back of her head.

"Of course we did," said Miriam. "He was very fussy about this matter of Mr Ramsbury settling on a profession."

"I wonder why," mused Judith. Though she was touched to learn that both her sister and her future brother-in-law had spoken on her behalf, she couldn't completely hide her frustration with her father.

Miriam finally sat up, rubbing her eyes.

"It's because Mama is dead," she said. "There's only Aunt Leah to help us if something happens to Papa before any of the boys have their own means. And as you're doubtless aware, the one thing Aunt Leah has never had is money."

Judith felt an instinctive sympathy for her father. Though she often worried about what might happen if Mrs Haddington withdrew her support for her father's position, rarely had she considered the possibility that he might die early. If he did, Miriam was correct that their family would be left with almost nothing. Judith had not asked, but she assumed that her sister would have five thousand pounds settled on her as well. If Judith and Miriam both took their dowries to their marriages, there would likely be nothing left for their brothers. And five thousand pounds, though considerable, could easily be lost in a bank failure or an investment scheme. Recent events had taught Judith that depending only on savings for one's future was a precarious business.

Plainly, the rector had considered those unfortunate possibilities and was doing all he could to protect his children's futures.

"Oh, Papa," said Judith. "Miriam, tell me honestly, has he been in good health?"

Her sister nodded. "Of course, but that is no guarantee for anyone. Just look at what happened to that poor young man, Mr Lush."

"We have no reason to think that Papa would be murdered!"

"No, but we never know when our last day on this earth will be. Such knowledge belongs to God."

Since Judith agreed completely, she could only quietly contemplate her father's decision. Perhaps it was not as unwise as she had originally thought. She resolved to speak to Morgan about it later, with some difficulty returning to her original intention in waking her sister.

"We have to speak with Joseph," said Judith.

Miriam shook her head, slouching as she did so. "And convince him to behave himself? We've all been trying, Judith. He never listens."

"He's had a shock," said Judith. "I've been away as often as I've been here, and now you are leaving as well."

"To marry, not to gallivant about the continent!"

Judith did not dignify that with an answer, though she did take a moment to think about the question of whether Russia was a part of Europe or Asia. In St Petersburg, she'd seen palaces of European design and a splendour that could likely rival anything in Vienna or Paris. She had also met people who spoke perfect French, waltzed beautifully, and yet possessed cultural sensibilities that were utterly strange to her. Perhaps the best answer would be that the Russia she knew belonged to both continents and also neither. But that was not a topic that would interest her sister.

"It may seem the same to Joseph," she said finally. "Moving to Russia, marrying."

Miriam scowled. "He's not a simpleton."

"No," agreed Judith. "But the women he loves most are not always with him."

They were silent, and Judith knew that Miriam was thinking of their mother. Her loss still gripped their hearts, as it always would. Judith knew that they would feel her absence even more keenly on the day of her sister's wedding.

"She warned me about marriage, you know," said Miriam, without needing to name their mother.

"It was her duty," said Judith, and she saw how her sister's face had fallen. "Oh, Miriam, I'm sure she would have loved Mr Barnwell. You need have no worries on that score."

But Miriam was lost in the memory. "She said that there was no easy escape so I must be very sure. Mama told me my husband could stray and I would have no recourse. And that the standards of accepted conduct from married men are so low that I might be shocked, were I ever to learn more about them."

Judith sighed. "She was a curate's wife, Miriam. She saw the worst of marriage almost constantly, as did Papa. But I'm sure she did not mean to keep you from marrying. She said similar things to me often, simply to keep me cautious."

Before they could say anything more about it, Aunt Leah came in, holding Joseph by the arm. He raced over and buried his head in Judith's side.

"You're getting tall," Judith said mildly, looking to Aunt Leah for an explanation.

Her aunt frowned, touching the boy's light and messy hair.

"He was shaking when he woke," she explained. "He had a nightmare."

"Come into my bed, you little scamp. You'll freeze," grumbled Miriam.

Judith gave Aunt Leah a nod, letting her know that she could leave. Aunt Leah understood, bending to kiss Joseph before she left the room. The little boy's agitation was greatest in a large party. With only his two sisters, he might calm himself more quickly.

"Joseph," said Judith, "as you know, I was away in Russia for a time."

"You're always away," said her brother, kicking the bedclothes aside with one foot, his arms folded. Miriam sat next to him in the bed, frowning at him with an expression of puzzlement and concern.

"I know I've been away at times," said Judith. "Often. I'm

often away," she said under the force of her brother's accusing glare.

"Moses and Aaron said you... weren't coming back." Joseph spoke so rapidly that Judith hardly understood him.

"What?" she said. "Never?"

But he said nothing.

"I'll always come back, and of course I shall always write," said Judith.

Still, Joseph only stared at her.

Miriam spoke gently to her brother. "You know that I am moving."

When he did not speak, she continued. "Mr Barnwell and I shall be settled near that inn where we catch the post," she told him.

Still, Joseph was silent, though a frown made itself known on his face.

"'Tis only fifteen miles," continued Miriam. "You could walk it all in a day, if you weren't so lazy."

She poked her brother's ribs, and to Judith's astonishment, Joseph smiled.

"Maybe two days, you're so slow," Miriam said. "You walk like an old barn cat."

"I do not," said Joseph, laughing as Miriam continued to tickle him.

"You do," she insisted.

"Will Joseph visit often? And will you come here often?" asked Judith, glancing carefully at her brother.

Miriam nodded solemnly. "I shall. I won't be far, but he is too lazy to visit me."

Joseph and Miriam both dissolved in laughter. Judith, still not sure whether she'd been forgiven for her long absences, did not join them.

But she did smile, even when she was summoned downstairs to see a visitor. Perhaps all would yet be well.

Louisa-Margaretta knew that she looked a fright. She had worn one of her best gowns, as she found that the trick nearly always helped her feel better after a sleepless night. It was not working, though. She knew very well that her complexion looked terrible and that her lips were set in a tight expression.

Judith knew better than to try to pry any answers out of her friend. She was very quiet for the first part of their walk, after Louisa-Margaretta refused to speak. Once they got to Wycliff Castle, Louisa-Margaretta went straight to the room where her mother sat writing her letters. She could feel Judith's unease. It was always difficult for Judith to be in the room with a woman who so openly disliked her.

Poor Judith! If she was apprehensive about the conversation, she would feel even worse when she heard Louisa-Margaretta's question.

First, there was the matter of closing the doors. Louisa-Margaretta also asked her mother to come sit by the fire, where the noise might drown out some of their conversation.

Mrs Haddington was amused but not unhappy. Though her greeting to Judith was rather strained, she touched Louisa-Margaretta's cheek affectionately.

"I haven't seen you up this early in at least a fortnight, my dear," she said.

"I didn't sleep," said Louisa-Margaretta.

Her mother frowned, her smile faltering. "Whatever is

the matter, dear? Mr Blackmore is recuperating quite well, I assure you—"

"Mr Blackmore!" said Louisa-Margaretta. "He has nothing to do with it. Only Mrs Crampton was so concerned about him breaking his marriage vows that she told me something about Papa."

Mrs Haddington was not smiling at all then. She made no response.

"Is it true?" asked Louisa-Margaretta.

Mrs Haddington sat down next to the fire. "Girls. Louisa-Margaretta, Judith. Come sit with me."

Judith edged closer, choosing a chair as far away from Mrs Haddington as possible. Louisa-Margaretta remained standing.

"Mrs Crampton said that Judith is the spitting image of Papa," she said. "That she looks like nobody in her own family except perhaps her mother."

Judith stood immediately, shaking her head. "I can hardly believe that of Mrs Crampton. Louisa-Margaretta, how can you repeat such a thing?"

"Is Papa Judith's father?" asked Louisa-Margaretta, speaking directly to her mother, who had not contradicted her.

Mrs Haddington took a deep breath. "Yes."

But even as she admitted it, Judith was already leaving.

37

Judith knew she would probably find Mr Haddington at breakfast. Like Louisa-Margaretta, he came down each morning expecting a hearty repast, and he would probably not vary his routine even after the excitement of the previous evening.

With every room she passed, Judith convinced herself that Mrs Crampton's conclusion could not possibly be true. After all, her mother was a kind and virtuous woman, devoted to both her husband and all her children.

A devoted mother would marry quickly in order to give her firstborn child a father. The thought came into Judith's head unbidden, and she endeavored to reject it.

A mirror hung in the passageway. Judith did not wish to look, but she was drawn to her reflection. Unlike Miriam, who greatly resembled their mother, Judith knew that she was not as handsome. She shared some of Mr Haddington's features. Most of all, she noticed her eyes. They were a muddy shade of brown. Her sister and brothers all had beautiful eyes in different hues of blue, as did both of her parents.

Mr Haddington had brown eyes.

Judith walked on, the confirmations flying into her mind quickly. Her father had a much greater income then, as a result of his lucrative position as rector, than he had ever enjoyed before. As soon as the Haddington family had moved to Derbyshire, they offered Judith's father the position, and he accepted. Thanks to their patronage, the St Clair family lived comfortably, at least as long as the living lasted.

But Judith had never questioned Mrs Haddington's choice of her father. That Mrs Haddington was a deeply religious woman, and that she had respect for her rector's learning and conviction, Judith had never doubted. But surely there were many such clergymen, some of them local to Derbyshire. For Mrs Haddington to choose a relative stranger then lavish him with a most lucrative patronage?

Even Mrs Haddington, though, might well be ignorant of the true circumstances. Only her husband could answer.

When Judith found Mr Haddington alone, she could not speak at first. Usually, the sight of her friend's father bent over a plate of eggs and meat would not have been arresting. But on that day, she could not help searching his features, wondering if even her knuckles somehow resembled his.

"Louisa-Margaretta told me that..." She found herself unable to finish. If her friend were mistaken, if somehow it was all a scheme of Mrs Crampton, the topic was too humiliating to broach.

But Mr Haddington put down his silverware. "I'm sorry we didn't tell you earlier. Your mother never wished it, nor Mr St Clair."

"My father," said Judith, her voice thin. "He is my father and will always be my father."

"Of course," said Mr Haddington. "I've no right, I know."

Judith fixed her gaze on a point outside the window. One of the branches on her favourite chestnut tree was waving in the cold gusts of wind. Judith did not know how to answer the man. He had once seemed so familiar that she was able to easily ignore him, but right then, she realised they knew very little of each other. They had probably never once had a genuine conversation.

"It has been delightful," he said. "Knowing you, coming to see your bond with your sister—"

"Stop," said Judith. She had always thought of Louisa-Margaretta as someone who was like a sister to her, not an actual sister. It seemed a mockery that they had lived for years, by then, in close proximity without knowing anything of their connection.

"I am going to leave Derbyshire," said Judith. "I don't wish to hear anything from any member of your family ever again."

Mr Haddington had tears in his eyes. Judith realised that she had never seen him cry. She strove to remain unmoved. However deep his pain, her heartbreak was greater.

"And I don't wish to have any of your money," she said. So the mysterious matter of the five thousand pounds that her father wished to settle on her was cleared up. Of course he had such a sum of money! It had no doubt come from her natural parent, not the person she still regarded and loved as a father.

"No," said Mr Haddington. "Please, I beg you."

"I will find a way to marry without it," said Judith, making no further attempt to stop her tears. "But I cannot accept it."

She left the room before she could truly weep. When she thought of the marriage portion of five thousand pounds, that was all the confirmation she needed that her father had known the truth all along. Indeed, he must have been aware from the moment of Judith's birth that she was not his natural child. That thought, had she followed it through, might have cheered her. She had never known anything from her father but love, affection, and genuine regard, though he had doubtless always been aware of her origins.

Instead, it was one more betrayal, and Judith found herself quite unable to face it. She would gladly have run all the way to the rectory, seeking only an empty room where she could curl up, if she had not heard a shriek almost as soon as she entered the passageway.

Mrs Blackmore was out of her bed but looking very ill indeed. "Help me," the young woman said.

"You're out of bed!" said Judith, so surprised that the tension in her throat eased.

"Yes, I wished to walk, but I can't now," moaned Mrs Blackmore. "Please, for God's sake, help me! At least help me to my bedchamber!"

Judith looked doubtfully at the young woman then sighed. "Take heart. I'll only be a moment."

She turned around and went into the breakfast room, where Mr Haddington was sobbing.

"Mr Haddington," Judith said, her voice clear and strong. She doubted she would ever call him anything else, but her vow never to speak with him again would have to be broken. "Please ring for help. Mrs Blackmore needs our assistance."

As soon as Mr Haddington rang for a servant, Judith went out to the place in the passageway where the young woman was slumped down against the wall.

"Let's get you up, then." She never would have been able to lift Mrs Blackmore, but Mr Haddington helped her. They took her to the nearest room, a sparsely furnished little parlor that the family seldom used.

"On your hands and knees," said Judith, the instructions coming to her by rote. "Let me push on your back, just here. Is that better?"

"Yes," gasped Mrs Blackmore. "A little higher."

Mr Haddington hesitated. "You have her, then? I will ring."

"Yes," said Judith. "Thank you."

Louisa-Margaretta went to her father, but before she could find him, she heard an animal cry of pain.

Looking into a seldom-used parlor, she saw Mrs Blackmore. The woman was supported by two servants, Judith at her back.

"Go and fetch Mrs Crampton," Judith was saying, no haste in her voice. "She'll have more remedies to offer. And we'll need more ladies to press on Mrs Blackmore's back during the pains. It could be days before the baby arrives."

"Days?" said Mrs Blackmore. "Not days. Not days, surely."

Judith smiled grimly, patting the young woman's neck with a damp handkerchief. "Yes, I'm afraid. But you'll get through it."

"I'll get Mrs Crampton," said Louisa-Margaretta. She did not wish to stay there, watching Mrs Blackmore suffer, but she found herself unable to step away immediately. Judith, who had always seemed utterly different, had been a blood relation all along. In some respects, she was the sister that Louisa-Margaretta had begged for.

Of course, Judith already had a sister. And no doubt, the

news would only drive Judith away from the Haddingtons, straight back to Miriam and all the other St Clairs.

Louisa-Margaretta longed to ask her friend what she thought of it all, but she was too ashamed. It was her father, after all, who had caused all the trouble. And in spite of that, her mother had stayed with him and gone on to have another child! She would never understand them.

"Thank you, Louisa-Margaretta," said Judith, her eyes still fixed on Mrs Blackmore.

Louisa-Margaretta understood the dismissal, and she left the room quickly.

She found old Mrs Crampton in Mama's bedchamber, of all places, having a hushed conference. While she guessed at the topic of their conversation, Louisa-Margaretta's cheeks burned, but she said only that Mrs Blackmore required assistance. Mrs Crampton was happy to go down to the young lady, though she repeated many of the same things that Judith had said. She appeared to be in no particular hurry. "It may be many days and nights. All our strength and efforts will be needed."

I hope she wasn't speaking about me," said Louisa-Margaretta, her face turning sour after Mrs Crampton left. "*I* certainly don't intend to go back into that room before Mrs Blackmore is quite finished."

Mrs Haddington's smile was gentle. "I'm sure there will be plenty of other ladies, dear."

When Louisa-Margaretta did not respond right away, Mrs Haddington continued. "I'm sure you have a lot of questions. And I apologise for keeping this from you. I wanted to respect the late Mrs St Clair's wishes, though I did question the decision many times."

Louisa-Margaretta could hear no more. "I need to go to one of my brothers," she said shortly. "Not to Percival and

Peggy, of course. Too many children. Or Augustus, they move too often. Perhaps Loftus."

Mrs Haddington plainly did not wish to refuse, but she was uncharacteristically silent. She must have been thinking of all Louisa-Margaretta's reasons for avoiding Percival. After the most recent revelation, being surrounded by a large, happy family might be taxing. Sherborne had only three children, and they were rather better behaved than Percival's unruly brood. Loftus had no children at all, and as a bachelor without a fixed occupation, he would have the most time to spend with Louisa-Margaretta.

Mama plainly did not approve. "I'm sure Sherborne and Clara would love to have you," she said at last. "I'll write to them straightaway. But Louisa-Margaretta, you must let me tell you more of the circumstances—"

"No," she said. "I will not hear of any such thing."

She left the room, ready to find her riding habit and call for a horse.

If nobody accompanied her that time, at least there would be no broken legs.

Her broken heart was cumbersome enough.

Mrs Crampton, Judith was discovering, was not a conventional woman.

She did not agree with the idea of keeping the birthing room dark and hot. Instead, she liked plenty of light, and she called for opening the windows when fresh air was needed. And in the evening, when Mrs Blackmore began to weep with frustration and anger, Mrs Crampton called for a walk.

"I can't walk," said Mrs Blackmore. "What of these pains?"

"Walking will get the baby out," said Mrs Crampton curtly. "If you stay on that couch, you'll go mad."

"Everyone will see me!" cried Mrs Blackmore.

Judith privately thought the young lady was right to be apprehensive. In spite of the hurried ministrations of Mrs Crampton, Mrs Guppy, Judith herself, and the series of maids who had been sent in to help with the birth, Mrs Blackmore looked a fright.

But Mrs Guppy, for the first time, burst into laughter. "It was impossible to fix your hair when you were younger. You used to fight like a wild animal! I'm sure I can do something with it now."

When the next wave of pain had passed, Mrs Guppy got to work. She was quick. Though Mrs Blackmore's simple braid, tucked beneath a cap, would not have been considered fashionable, it was certainly respectable.

"Let's get you into the other gown," said Mrs Guppy. "It's comfortable enough, and nobody will be observing you, my dear."

After Mrs Blackmore had been made presentable, she sank into a chair and leaned on the bed as the pain took her once again. One of the younger maids pushed at Mrs Blackmore's back like one who had been born to it. They were in such a rhythm then, Mrs Blackmore no longer cried out in pain each time, though Judith could see that she was exhausted.

"A walk will get your spirits up," said Mrs Crampton. "You'll soon see."

They made a strange party, the ladies traipsing through Wycliff Castle. At first, Mrs Blackmore's steps were uncertain. One day in the little room and she was already like a confined animal, scared to venture beyond its bounds. But she soon regained her feeling of freedom as well as her sense of purpose.

"How does my husband?" she asked, panting a bit as she quickened her steps. "Tell me of his recovery."

Mrs Guppy shook her head. "Nothing you need concern yourself with, dear. He isn't having a baby! He went riding off in the woods for no good reason, faster than he could manage, and it's no surprise he hurt himself."

Mrs Crampton took the other woman's arm, keeping her quiet as she addressed Mrs Blackmore directly.

"Much better," she said. "I daresay he has learned something from his ordeal already. Would you like to see him?"

"Yes," panted Mrs Blackmore. "I don't want to go up all those stairs, but he can hardly come see me, can he?"

"That's the spirit," said Mrs Crampton.

"Don't worry about the stairs," Judith added. "You've no reason to come down again. You may stay in your own room, or any other upstairs room, if they're too much for you."

Mrs Blackmore gave a high-pitched laugh. "And see a better view than the one I have been staring at for a day! I didn't even think of that, Miss St Clair."

Mrs Blackmore then sank to her knees, and Mrs Guppy cried out. The pain seemed no worse than before. After it had passed, young Mrs Blackmore stood again.

Judith stood behind the young woman on the stairs. Mrs Crampton didn't seem concerned at all, but Judith was sure that Mrs Blackmore would either pitch forward, crushing her baby, or lean back, tumbling down the stairs. But she held fast to the railing at the side and did not seem troubled. She simply counted each stair, sounding every bit like a young child learning arithmetic for the first time.

Finally, they reached the top, and Mrs Blackmore's pace

quickened. She had to stop again in the hallway due to the pain. Judith, who was already directly behind her, pressed on Mrs Blackmore's back. But there was a change in the party. Mrs Guppy no longer wept with concern for her daughter, the maids were impressed, and Mrs Crampton seemed relieved, though of course, she had never let on that she'd been worried at all.

"Nancy," said Mr Blackmore.

Judith noticed that he was attended only by one of the village ladies, summoned by Mrs Haddington to be a nursemaid for the Blackmore baby. It appeared she was going to be a nursemaid for the baby's father first. There was a pot of tea next to him but no wine, and he had been reading by candlelight.

"George," said Mrs Blackmore, her voice tremulous.

"How are you?" they asked at the same time.

Mrs Blackmore smiled shyly. "As you see."

But then she was overtaken again. She went forward, on her knees, her arms up on the side of the bed as she buried her face in the coverlet. Mrs Crampton, in spite of her age, got to Mrs Blackmore first and pressed on her back. But it was a long one. Judith had noticed the periods of pain becoming longer and more frequent.

By the end of it, Mrs Blackmore was crying, her shoulder stooped with exhaustion, and Mrs Guppy's face had hardened in disapproval.

"Gentlemen ought never to see this," she said. "Nancy, come along."

"No," said Mr Blackmore. He could reach only one of his wife's hands, but he drew her to him. "Nancy, you are so strong. So much stronger than I am."

Mrs Blackmore's exhausted face lightened a bit. "Yes, I should say so," she agreed, and the whole party laughed.

"Come, give them a moment," said Mrs Crampton. "Mrs Guppy can stay."

She shepherded Judith out with the maids, and they stood at the end of the hall. It was hardly likely to be a romantic scene, what with the young woman's mother present the whole time, the young man not able to move, much less stand, and the birthing pains interrupting any conversation.

But as Judith walked out, she noticed that Mrs Blackmore was holding her husband's hand, whispering something to him that made them both laugh.

38

"You ought to get some sleep," said Mrs Crampton. "You should go back to the rectory, Miss St Clair. But before you do, there was someone who wished to speak with you."

She gave a nod down the passageway, where Morgan was standing.

"I've asked for a tray instead of dinner," he said, a nervous smile on his face. "I couldn't face the meal. How is she?"

"Well enough," said Judith. "It is not an easy birth, as it's her first, but Mrs Crampton says there's nothing we need to worry about now."

They conversed in hushed tones in the passageway.

"We should go to the music room," decided Morgan. "I've some news to share."

They walked in silence without needing to discuss anything. Both knew it was safer not to speak of anything important at Wycliff Castle until they were quite sure that they would be alone. Morgan seemed elated, which troubled Judith. She was going to have to spoil what was probably a long-held illusion about one of his most admired relatives. Even when they reached the music room, she had no idea how she would tell him what she had learned about Mr Haddington.

"I admit, I was impatient when you were with Mrs Blackmore," said Morgan. "Only, I felt I could not interrupt."

"Before you tell me," said Judith, "I have news of my own, and I'm afraid it's very troubling."

At first, she had trouble speaking, but Morgan gave her the time she needed to compose her thoughts. Best start with the money, she decided. That was the least difficult to speak of and the most relevant.

"I will no longer be receiving five thousand pounds upon my marriage, regardless of the exact circumstances," Judith said. "It was not my father's money, it belonged to the Haddingtons, and I have refused it."

She knew that an explanation must follow and dreaded having to give it. But instead of shock, she saw only resignation in Morgan's face.

"I am sorry," he said. "This has to do with Mr Haddington, then?"

Judith's hands, which she had attempted to keep in her lap, sprang to the table. She could not believe her beloved's reaction. "You knew," she said slowly.

"No," he said. "Nothing was certain at all. Only, certain men in the family speculated. Rumours, that's all they were."

"And you said nothing to me," Judith said.

All at once, she was reminded of that first betrayal. Morgan had known for months that, as a Quaker, it would be difficult or impossible for him to enter into marriage with

Miss Judith St Clair, the rector's daughter. And yet, in spite of every opportunity, it was only when he began speaking seriously of marriage that he had raised that barrier. Judith, while shocked and upset that religion would force her apart from a man she had come to love and respect, was also angry that he had kept such an important secret.

And now, it appeared, the pattern had re-emerged.

"You would have taken his money, married me, and still never told me," she said, disbelieving.

"No!" said Morgan. "Mr Haddington is a good man, and I didn't think idle talk was worth repeating."

"Then you're saying that there are others in the family who know," said Judith faintly. She began remembering comments herself. Nothing overtly disrespectful but observations about the color of her eyes, her father's position in Derbyshire, and even her relationship with Louisa-Margaretta. More than one person had referred to the two of them as sisters. Judith had always supposed that that was a slip of the tongue, but perhaps it was only an acknowledgement of what was clear to everyone else on earth.

"I never knew anything for certain, not until today," said Morgan. "And of course we don't have to accept the money if those are your feelings. I came to tell you about a position that I was offered. The letter came yesterday, but in all the confusion—"

Judith held up a hand, and her voice faltered. "I am not sure we ought to be married," she said. "I congratulate you on the position."

The shock on Morgan's face almost broke her resolve, and she took a deep breath. "I need to think about this. I need to pray."

"Of course," he said, but she could see he was devastated. He reached out to take her hand but stopped himself, which quite broke Judith's heart.

Instead of giving him a proper farewell, she simply left the room, deciding that she ought to go back to Mrs Blackmore. It would have been impossible to stay.

39

After the evening meal was over, Miss Guppy and Miss Blackmore both stated they would be going to bed early in case their presence was needed later. Louisa-Margaretta could tell they were lying. Poor ladies, they probably just wanted to hide so they wouldn't have to deal with any of the birthing nonsense.

Louisa-Margaretta felt the same, except she wouldn't hide. She would simply refuse.

But there was no hiding from Mama, who was the only other lady in the party after the gentlemen went off together. And she would not let Louisa-Margaretta escape. In the music room, she carefully shut the doors then drew her daughter to the chilly window. The house was almost silent. They could not hear Mrs Blackmore, and Louisa-Margaretta hoped that the poor woman was sleeping.

"You can go to Sherborne and Clara," Mrs Haddington said, sounding more like her imperious self. "I've sent an express, but I'm quite sure they'll agree to it. You may leave as soon as you like."

Louisa-Margaretta knew her mother well. "On what condition?"

"You will hear me out," said her mother. "You do not have to speak, only listen."

Louisa-Margaretta frowned. "And you'll let me go tomorrow, if I like?"

"Stay for Christmas," said Mrs Haddington curtly. "I don't ask for much, Louisa-Margaretta. But I ask for this."

Louisa-Margaretta privately disagreed with the first part of that statement, but she knew she was trapped. She was not going to run away from Wycliff Castle with no money, after all.

Mrs Haddington did not need any more encouragement. She began to tell her story.

"When your father and I were newlyweds, we were happy together. Very happy, in fact. He did not spare himself when it came to ensuring my every comfort. Then we had our first child, and we were immediately entranced. Augustus was an easy baby, so quiet and lovely. But the children came fast after that, and it was a time when your father's professional interests were expanding. He poured his heart into his work to ensure a comfortable future for me and for the boys, but I resented the lack of attention that it left for us. When I gave birth to Loftus, I thought I would lose my mind and felt very melancholy for at least a year after.

"There were much greater demands on your father's business just as the demands on my own time and energy were at their height. I had four boys under the age of eight, and though I was determined never to have another child, I was exhausted. Your father was wonderful with the boys—he got all their energy out in a way that I could never match—but he was in Manchester for weeks at a time. And then he was in Manchester even more often, starting that spring or summer, but I hardly noticed. When he did come home to London, I was angry with him, and I tried to make him go to every opera and party with me, simply to make up for the absences, though I knew he hated it.

"It was 1785, then, the year, at Christmas, when he told me. I have always tried to make this season a holy and special time for our family, you see, since it holds such unpleasant associations for your father and me.

"Your papa had taken up with an actress. It was the first and last time such a thing happened. She was great with child, though not in the same manner as Mary, of course. This was no Christmas story, and she would have the child in rented rooms, not a manger. I hated the very thought of the woman, but your father had a surprising story. This actress had thrown him over, deciding to marry a clergyman rather than live as a rich man's mistress. That, I had to respect, though I was immediately suspicious of her motives.

"So I met the woman who was to become Mrs St Clair, and I must say, I could not hate her nearly as much as I meant to. I saw from the first how much she loved the man who was to become her husband and how he genuinely adored her. He wasn't simply thinking of himself as a saint, rushing in to save a fallen woman, giving her child a name. And to my great shock, they did not want any money for the child. The woman only made us promise that we would help the babe should something happen to her. As long as she was living, she said, she would see to it that no demands were placed on us. And she was as good as her word.

"In 1786, then, your father came back to the family for good. He dropped some of his business obligations or hired others to take care of them, and he was with us much more often from then on. Oh, I did not forgive him right away. But eventually, his apologies and my own good sense won out. I believed then, and I was right to think it, that we might have many happy years in our future. Less than a year later, you were born, after I had prayed for a daughter. And I knew that our family was complete.

"I know what you expected, Louisa-Margaretta. I could have refused to forgive your father, we could have lived separately, as so many married couples do. The possibility certainly crossed my mind. Yes, I was in the grip of melancholia, and there were many times when I was unkind, but I did not believe that I was to blame for your father's transgressions. I still do not believe that. There are many wronged wives who ought never to forgive their husbands. But I also think that forgiveness comes from God, and when it is in our power to extend it, that is a part of the divine in us."

[Ornamental Break?]

It was a pretty enough story, but Louisa-Margaretta was not in a forgiving mood.

"You have told me everything, then," she said sharply. "I shall leave the day after Christmas."

"Louisa-Margaretta," said her mother, but Louisa-Margaretta shook her head.

"You have said enough, Mama," she said. "You should leave me now."

40

The baby came in the early morning. Judith and Mrs Crampton roused Miss Guppy and Miss Blackmore, that they might take turns sleeping. Mrs Haddington was also present, though she tactfully kept out of sight when Judith was in the room. Judith knew that under other circumstances, Mrs Haddington would have wanted to be present for the entire time. But Judith could not feel grateful.

When the baby began to cry, Judith hid her own tears. All of a sudden, she remembered that she was a stranger and that Mrs Blackmore would probably not even remember her presence. Mrs Guppy took the baby immediately before sitting next to the mother, who was too exhausted to hold the little one but delighted in stroking her head.

"A little girl," she murmured. "We'll have to find a name for you."

Miss Guppy sat at her sister's other side, one arm around her shoulders. Her disgust with the process had gradually transformed into awe, and she smiled at the baby. Next to her, on a chair, Miss Blackmore admired her niece.

"So much hair!" she said. "She's beautiful."

Judith slipped away, certain that the little family would be able to manage. She ached for her own bed. As soon as the baby was born, she started thinking of how much she despised Wycliff Castle, how lovely it would be to walk out its elegant doors and never return. Some part of her knew that she would have to be reconciled to visiting the rectory, for as long as her father stayed, she would not be able to avoid it entirely. But as for the Haddingtons, she had no desire to see any of them again.

"Come and see the sanctuary," said Miriam. "Everything is ready for Christmas."

Judith sat in the parlour, staring at her brothers without seeing them. Nothing moved her to go see the seasonal decorations. She ought to have been happy, she supposed, or at least relieved. Ever since her conversation with Joseph, his temper had improved markedly. He was still quick to cry, but he recovered his spirits more easily. Moses and Aaron had stopped avoiding him, and all three brothers were engaged in the absorbing task of figuring out which type of Christmas greenery was the most prickly. Though Judith would normally have encouraged them to avoid any activity which involved blood, seeing the three of them play together warmed her heart.

"I'll see it on Christmas, then," said Judith. "Unless you need me there tonight."

Miriam frowned. "Surely you wouldn't want to miss Christmas Eve," she said doubtfully.

She and Judith had not discussed the question of the latter's parentage since Judith had mentioned it briefly. Judith, for the first time, was very glad that Miriam was going to be married. Let her mull over the subject with her future husband—it was too painful for Judith to raise.

"The Haddingtons?" said Miriam. "You don't have to see them, not if you don't wish to."

Judith did not respond, she only followed Miriam mutely out of the rectory. The day had dawned crisp and clear.

"You know that you'll always be a St Clair," said Miriam, opening one of the heavy front doors of the church for Judith, who wondered only briefly why they were entering that way. "You are still Mama and Papa's child, Judith. And my sister."

Judith felt a swell of emotion. She nodded at Miriam. "You are soon to become a Barnwell, though, not a St Clair."

Miriam could not resist a grin. "Christopher will never be my sister. And for all the time he's spent with us, he did miss the first two decades we had together. I'll always be Miriam St Clair first."

Judith nodded. In spite of her pain, she still felt a distant chime of pleasure to see her sister so happy.

"I'll leave you here," murmured Miriam, rushing to leave the sanctuary just as Judith realised she was not alone. A man stood in the middle of the aisle, not far from the entrance.

"You must forgive your sister," said Morgan. "She and Mr Barnwell have been spending as much time as they can with me."

He opened the door to the elaborate pew that Mrs Haddington had insisted be reserved for guests. Not only the guests of Wycliff Castle but also people who visited the poorest visitors. The Haddingtons' own pew, while grand, was no better than that one.

Morgan took a seat inside the pew, leaving the door open, but Judith did not follow.

"I am sorry," he said. "Perhaps an ambush was not quite correct. Miriam insisted."

Judith stood in the center aisle, by the door to the guest pew. It was probably the most proper place for her to stand. Though, of course, if she and Morgan were no longer an engaged couple, it was highly improper for them to be alone in the sanctuary at all. But she could not be sure.

"Miriam can be very stubborn," said Judith carefully.

Morgan smiled. "Well, I ought to be thankful that she's on my side, then. If she had taken against me, I don't think I would have been allowed to stay at Haddington Castle, much less approach the rectory, ever again."

His face grew serious. "Dear Judith," he said. "Please forgive me. In attempting to do justice to a man I admired, I failed you. And to a lesser degree, I failed my cousin."

"How is Louisa-Margaretta?" Judith could not stop herself from asking. She wanted nothing to do with Wycliff Castle, but she had been thinking of her friend. During the past week, Judith had concluded that her mother had been foolish. However, in taking up with a married man, she had not broken a vow. The greatest wrong had been committed by Mr Haddington. Even if infidelity was a sin common to many men, she knew that Louisa-Margaretta would not forgive it easily.

"She will not speak with me," said Morgan. "They say she is going away to stay with one of her brothers."

"Which brother? Oh, Sherborne, I'm sure," mused Judith before Morgan could answer. "She would have preferred to stay with Loftus, and her mother will have refused."

Both of them smiled briefly, then Judith grew serious again.

"I trust you not to indulge in gossip," she said. "But when there is some knowledge that must be shared, I wish you would not keep it from me either."

"I can solemnly promise never to do so again," said Morgan. "Oh, Judith, I am a selfish man. If I had known what the consequences would be for you, I would have repeated everything straightaway rather than lose you."

Judith swallowed. She came into the guest pew and sat down, though a distance remained between her and Morgan.

"You told me that you had news," she said. "We might begin with that."

He took that as an assurance that they had resumed their understanding, which Judith could not help thinking was a rather presumptuous interpretation. But seeing his wide smile, she did not wish to correct him either.

"I thought of it when we were speaking about education," he said. "There is a Quaker school very near London, and they need another teacher. I have told them of our marriage, and they will provide us with thirty pounds a year, coal, and a place to live. And all our meals, of course, provided we eat with the students."

Judith was privately horrified by the idea of taking all her meals with a group of students, but she did not wish to ruin the news by saying so.

"Well, I suppose without the five thousand pounds, such a position is no longer a requirement," she said. Seeing Morgan's face fall, she hastened to add, "But I think it is a very wise idea. And I'm sure I should love to go with my father's blessing."

He moved closer to her on the bench. "You are sure, then, Judith? You still wish to marry?"

She could feel her face breaking into a smile. "Of course I do."

41

They had to hold the wedding first thing in the morning on the last day of the year. Since the law decreed that the marriage must take place between eight in the morning and noon, it was easiest to ensure that it happened before any parishioners arrived. After all, it was a small party. Mr Barnwell's family lived far away, so it was only the St Clair family, Mr Morgan Ramsbury, and one of the Fletcher boys.

That final guest made Judith nervous.

"Should we have asked Mr Barnwell not to invite him, do you think?" she asked Morgan, standing close to him so her brothers would not hear.

"It would've been rather unfortunate if poor Mr Barnwell had no friend of his own here," Morgan responded. "Besides, I am sure we ought not to visit the sins of the father on the son."

"I don't know about sins," said Judith. "Pride, perhaps. Has the magistrate said anything to you?"

There was still plenty of talking in the sanctuary. Miriam

had not yet appeared, and the small group was growing restless.

"I should go look for her," Judith murmured just as Morgan answered.

"He has not addressed me directly, but I gather Mrs Haddington took her carriage to his home yesterday."

Judith gave a wry smile. "Yes, that sounds like something she would do. I suppose she demanded that he drop his inquiries?"

"No, she didn't. But she did go on quite a bit about the Blackmore baby. Lucy, they're calling her, Lucy Blackmore. Mrs Haddington uses her kindness to shame people into doing as she likes."

"And will it work with Mr Fletcher? Surely he considers his duties as a magistrate more important than a plump little baby."

"Apparently, no evidence of a single party's guilt has been put before him. It is just possible, Mrs Haddington claims, that Mr Lush fell on the needle somehow."

Judith shook her head. "Surely even she does not believe that."

"No, but Mr Fletcher does not wish to see his own reputation tarnished by false accusations again. I think we can trust him to be very cautious."

Judith looked at the aisle again. Miriam was nowhere in sight, but Judith had to get confirmation from Morgan. "The magistrate has told you that you can leave? With me?"

"Yes, Mrs Haddington was very firm on that point, apparently. She cares a great deal about your future."

Judith could not yet forgive the woman who had been so rude to her, all the while knowing of their family connection. Though part of her supposed that it was a reason for

Mrs Haddington's brusque manner, the enduring shame of having her husband's illegitimate child living within a stone's throw of her vast home.

Not illegitimate, Judith told herself. According to the law, her birth was absolutely legitimate, and she was her father's daughter. Judith St Clair, daughter of a respected clergyman.

And indeed, the sight of him standing there, perfectly calm as he waited to marry his daughter off, filled her heart with joy.

Judith walked up to him, taking care not to let any nerves show on her own face.

"Papa," she whispered. "Why does Miriam not come?"

"I cannot be sure," said her father.

"We must go to her," said Judith.

They found Miriam in the rectory, sitting in front of her mirror. She was not crying, but her expression was pensive.

"Your Mr Barnwell is waiting," said Judith. "Why do you sit here?"

"Because Mama told me not to get married," said Miriam. "At the very least, she said to be exceedingly cautious."

Mr St Clair looked at his daughters. Judith had not asked him directly about the story of her birth. The very thought of such a discussion pained her, but her father began telling the story himself.

"I have not wanted to speak with either of you about that gossip Mrs Crampton spread," he said. "She thought herself justified, I am sure, but there were many reasons your mother did not wish you to know."

"Well, they can hardly mean much to us now," said Judith. "It's too late, Papa."

"It is," agreed her father. "But I may at least explain to

you why your mother cautioned you against marriage, at least in general terms."

Miriam still looked sad, but she leaned her head to one side, listening intently. Judith pulled up a chair beside her sister, holding her hand.

"As you know," he said, "your mother's family had almost no money throughout her life. Perhaps you do not understand how poor they were, as it was not something she liked to discuss. My family did not have great resources, but neither were we hungry. Your mother's difficulties were much greater."

When neither of his daughters made to reply right away, he continued on.

"Her arrangement, then, with a wealthy patron, it was not something that she despised. Her very existence was so precarious, such a thing was to be celebrated, at least in her mind. But afterwards, her perspective began to change. She realised how very carefully we had to guard the secret. If she acquired any sort of reputation for licentiousness, though she was blameless as a young wife and mother, it could completely ruin my own prospects. And the man who was at the root of it all, he was married. Even if he were to be completely found out, he would face little or no consequences."

"She didn't want me to become a wronged wife like Mrs Haddington," said Miriam, brightening. "Well, I don't have many worries on that score."

"And if either of you ever does," said Mr St Clair, still exceedingly solemn, "you may always come home. A scandal is never worth avoiding if you must sacrifice your safety or your happiness."

Judith felt the weight of that pronouncement. Miriam, it

seemed, did not. However, she straightened her back and smiled.

"We've no time to waste, then," she said. "Time for me to get married."

42

Louisa-Margaretta's parents cornered her after the dinner on New Year's Eve. She had managed to escape the church service, passed most of the day riding, and provided the requisite amount of cooing about little Lucy Blackmore at the table. Nobody, she felt, knew her well enough to notice her low spirits. Miss Blackmore and Miss Guppy were, oddly enough, both fairly friendly, but they did not push past Louisa-Margaretta's low spirits when she made it clear that she wished to be left alone.

But Mama and Papa were a different matter. And united, they were formidable. They came into Louisa-Margaretta's bedchamber, where she had been lying still, and spoke to her.

"I hope you're not going to miss First Footing," said Mrs Haddington with forced cheer. "Such a charming custom!"

"And strange," offered Mr Haddington.

Louisa-Margaretta made no response.

"We can't go on this way forever, dear," said Mrs Haddington. "I know it all seems very recent to you, but you are trying to quarrel over events in the distant past."

"I learned of it only recently," said Louisa-Margaretta, "and only from a stranger."

Mr Haddington sighed. His wife sat down on the bed, touching her daughter's hair.

"My dear, would you have liked the news any better if we had told you many years ago?"

"No," said Louisa-Margaretta.

"Well, then," said Mrs Haddington. "You are now aware, and you needn't dwell on it, dear. The less is said, the better, as it is certainly best for this not to become generally known."

That response infuriated Louisa-Margaretta.

"This is the reason I do not plan on forgiving either of you," she said. "You brought me here to avoid a marriage that you did not like. At the time, I thought that your own reputations were spotless. Though I did not agree, at least you were pretending that my engagement to Isaac would be the first scandal our family had ever faced."

"There was no scandal when your friend Judith was born," said Mrs Haddington firmly. "We were very careful about that."

"I'm sure you were," said Louisa-Margaretta, her voice heavy with contempt. She found it exhausting, being so angry with her parents. Without Judith's company, and with Morgan distracted by the final days of his very long engagement, she had no companions at all.

But she could not forgive them.

"You may as well go," said Louisa-Margaretta, trying to suppress a tear as she turned away from her mother.

Her parents left, and Louisa-Margaretta sighed. Finally, she would be free of all the celebrations, and she could go see Sherborne and his family. Perhaps she would call on all of her old friends. There must be some way that she could keep going.

And Isaac is in London, she thought, but she suppressed that hope immediately. She must be mad, thinking about falling in love with another married man! Though in her heart, she knew that she was never in love with Mr Blackmore and that she would always love Isaac. She would do well to avoid him, then. Perhaps she could amend her conduct, in view of the shocking revelation about Judith. Old Mrs Crampton would get her way.

Louisa-Margaretta sighed, lying back in her bed and pulling a pillow over her eyes. It was simply no use trying not to think about Isaac. She always thought of him, whether he was with her or not. Those memories of her early days with him at the museum, looking at art and curiosities, would go to the grave with her.

But as she reflected on the museum itself, a memory came to her. Of course! Judith, having paid more attention to Madame Chatel, their painter friend, had remembered the pretty little painting that Mr Lush admired. When he corrected her as to the geography, Judith had simply blushed, murmuring that she must be mistaken. But Louisa-Margaretta had remembered watching Madame Chatel create that painting.

"I prefer landscapes to portraits," the Frenchwoman had stated, "when the subject of the portrait is not to my liking."

At the time, Louisa-Margaretta had only been interested in the reason that Madame Chatel disliked the Duke whom she was painting. Later on, she had concentrated on divining whether Madame Chatel had the makings of the killer. But Judith had been interested in the painting itself, and on reflection, Louisa-Margaretta vaguely remembered Madame Chatel leaving it as a gift for her hosts. As Judith had correctly stated, the landscape was a portrayal of some bit of coastline in France.

Louisa-Margaretta flung aside the pillow and strode out into the passageway. All the activity was near the entrance of the home, of course. Her mother would have made some arrangement for First Footing. Though there were few true strangers in the village, there was bound to be some visitor whom the Haddingtons had not yet met. As long as that person was first to cross the threshold in the New Year, all of Wycliff Castle would enjoy good fortune. Or so the superstition went, anyway. Mrs Haddington generally dragged the poor soul inside and stood with them under what she had termed her "Praying Ball," which rather ruined the whole celebratory feeling.

But that evening, it was all quite convenient for Louisa-Margaretta. She went to the room where the painting was, finding it without any trouble. It took a moment to get at the thing, but she was tall, and by dragging a table over, she could just reach it. After that, it was easy for Louisa-Margaretta to find her cousin's little watch, wrapped in an old rag and secured to the back of the painting with some glue.

"I'm sorry, Mr Lush," she murmured. "You're not nearly as clever as you thought you were."

It gave her some gratification to think that such a statement could apply to many of the men of her acquaintance. Even though Judith's mind was the nimblest, Louisa-Margaretta could often solve puzzles, and she longed to share that particular solution with her friend.

After she had held the watch for a moment, her triumph turned to anguish. Her parents had promised a carriage to Morgan and Judith, but they had refused to accept the offer, under the circumstances. Judith's pride was a force to be reckoned with. So the young couple were traveling post, with a servant, staying separately until they could have the Quaker wedding.

Louisa-Margaretta, of course, was not invited.

She thought of all her plans for weddings. When Louisa-Margaretta thought that she would marry, Judith was going to come to hers. When her friend and cousin planned to marry, Louisa-Margaretta had always been sure that she would be included. Now, neither would come to pass, and she had no way even to help them by passing along Cousin Morgan's final treasure.

But instead of weeping, with steely determination, she let her fist curl around the watch.

"Someday," she whispered, thinking of her friend Judith. Not her friend, really, her sister.

"Someday, I will give this back to you."

TWO LADIES AND A MANHUNT

ALSO BY EVE TARRINGTON

Two Spinsters and a Corpse

Two Spinsters and a Duel

Two Spinsters and a Madman

Two Spinsters Books 1-3 Box Set

Two Spinsters and a Thief

Two Spinsters and an Assassin

Two Spinsters and a Villain

ABOUT THE AUTHOR

Eve Tarrington is a Jane Austen fanatic. She has written dozens of books, but this is her first historical mystery set in the Regency era. She is thankful to her readers, her family, and her friends.

Would you like to know when Eve Tarrington is putting out a new novel? You're in luck! Join the mailing list at tenaciousteacuppress.com/eveTnews. You'll get an email when a new book is coming out.

In addition, you'll get a special copy of *Two Ladies and a Manhunt*, a subscriber bonus that follows young Judith and Louisa-Margaretta as they separately search for a young lady. When Louisa-Margaretta's friend disappears from one of the most exclusive London ballrooms shortly after coming out, suspicions and false accusations fly. For very different reasons, Judith and Louisa-Margaretta, still strangers, are intent on finding her killer.

www.ingramcontent.com/pod-product-compliance
Lightning Source LLC
LaVergne TN
LVHW040047080526
838202LV00045B/3533